The
Jumping-Off Place

AT THE END OF THE BARN A DOOR HAD BEEN CUT

The
Jumping-Off Place

Marian Hurd McNeely

Illustrated by
William Siegel

Dover Publications, Inc.
Mineola, New York

Bibliographical Note

This Dover edition, first published in 2017, is an unabridged republication of the work originally published by Longmans, Green and Co., New York, in 1929.

International Standard Book Number

ISBN-13: 978-0-486-81568-8
ISBN-10: 0-486-81568-4

Manufactured in the United States by LSC Communications
81568401   2017
www.doverpublications.com

TO THE TWO
WHO WERE THERE WITH ME

CONTENTS

ILLUSTRATIONS

CHAPTER I

WHERE THE WEST BEGINS

DOWN on their knees, a boy and girl were taking up the kitchen linoleum. It was a queer time to be at that work — half-past eight in the evening — and there was an air of strangeness about the house; an unusual silence, a hollowness and a fragrance of crushed flowers in the air. The lighted candle, which had been set on the floor to piece out the electric light, shone on the towsled, red head of the boy and on the firm lips of his sister, who was working on the opposite side of the room.

The Linville kitchen was usually the noisiest room in the house, but tonight it was so still that the "plack" of the tacks, and an occasional grunt over a stubborn fastening, were the only sounds. It was not often that fifteen and seventeen worked together so silently or so soberly. As they approached each other along the sides of the room there was a cough and a step on the back porch, and someone tried the door. Both young people sat up, looking as though caught in the act.

"Aunt Jule!" whispered Becky.

"You *bet* it's Aunt Jule," said Dick. "Come back to see if we've read the will."

"I know she expected to be asked to stay to supper this afternoon," commented his sister. "But I did hope we'd be alone tonight. I suppose we've got to let her in."

"You haven't told her we were going?"

There was an insistent knock on the door.

Becky shook her head. "No, I knew she'd make a fuss about it and I didn't want Uncle Jim bothered when he was so sick. But she might as well know now. Unlock the door, Dick."

"I'd rather let in measles," growled the boy.

The visitor stepped over the threshold with a word of commendation, which was an unusual entrance for her. "You children are wise to keep the door locked," she said. "You can't be too careful, now that you're all alone. I never pick up a paper that I don't read of a house being robbed somewhere."

Aunt Jule was fifty-nine and unyielding. The stiff clothes of 1910 were made for her type. Her black hair was drawn tightly over a stiff pompadour roll; her shirt waist was starchy; and in temperament she was like both hair and waist.

"This is a fine to-do," she said, from the doorway. "I come up here to talk over the services and cheer you up and I find you tearing the house down, in those filthy overalls. What if company drops in? What you doing in those clothes the day of a funeral, anyway? I don't think you're paying much respect to your dead uncle."

"Oh, yes, we are," answered Dick. "He told us to get the linoleum up as soon as he was gone. 'That's one job I'll skip,' he said. 'I always despised taking out tacks.'" He smiled at the speech that brought Uncle Jim so near, but his eyes were ready to overflow. "We can't pull tacks in Sunday clothes."

"Better not let anyone else see you grinning that way," advised his aunt, taking a chair. "Of course Jim would make jokes on his death bed, but the day of a funeral is no time to repeat them. Why on earth are you children upsetting the house, this way?"

"We're turning the linoleum," said Dick, sourly.

Becky gave her brother a reproving look. "We're getting ready to pack, Aunt Julia."

"To pack?" exclaimed Aunt Jule. "For what?"

"For Dakota."

"Dakota! You aren't planning to go out to the Jumping-off Place to visit that homestead?"

"No," said Dick. "Not to visit it, but to live on it."

Aunt Jule gasped. "I thought that idea died when your Uncle Jim did. Or rather, when he was first taken sick. He must have known, after the first week of his stroke, that he never could farm again."

Becky's eyes filled with tears. "Yes, he knew it. He told us so just after his speech came back to him."

"Well," said Aunt Jule, triumphantly, "That put an end to it."

"It put an end to it for him, but not for us. He wanted us to go on without him." Becky's lips trembled, but her voice was resolute.

"He must have been delirious."

"Oh, no, he wasn't. He called Dick and me into his room as soon as he could speak, and talked it over with us. He told us he knew that he was never going to be well again and that it was up to us to 'run the engine alone.' He asked us if we thought that we could hold down the claim for fourteen months for the sake of a good farm, some day. And we told him we could. Even Phil and Joan promised him that they'd help."

"The man was certainly out of his head."

Becky's eyes flashed. "He never was saner in his life, Aunt Jule. He told us all about his plans, just what we'd have to pay for the land now, and what he thought it would be worth in ten years. He told us that if we were willing to put in fourteen months of hard work the claim would give each one of us a good schooling. He planned the whole trip for us. He had me bring him pencil and a note-book, and he kept them by the side of his bed all the time he was sick. And as he thought of things he'd either write them himself, or else have me jot them down: just how we were to go, what we would need to take, how we were to get started, how much land we were to have broken, what we were to plant, what clothes we would want — there wasn't a thing that he didn't plan for."

"And his idea was for you children to go out alone, and live alone until you proved up?"

"Yes, it was." Becky went resolutely back to her linoleum.

"I can't believe he was himself. People often get those queer notions when they're sick."

"Well, I can prove to you that he *was* himself," said Dick hotly. "After he had most everything planned he said to us: 'There's only one thing that worries me. I'm not afraid that you can't settle the land — you kids; but who's going to settle your fights?' Now, does that sound as if Uncle Jim were sane or not?"

Tears sprang to Becky's eyes at the dear, familiar phrasing. Aunt Jule nodded grimly. "Well, I admit it does," she said, "But I can't see what he was thinking about. You children, being orphans, have picked up some things about helping yourselves, but you've never tried running a house alone in your lives, even in a civilized community where there are churches and grocery stores. And to go out in that God-forsaken place, among dirty Indians and coyotes, with nothing growing but sage brush, would be new business for you. Jim himself told me that the nearest neighbor lived a quarter of a mile away. What would you do if you were sick? There's always chills and fever in new country."

"Take quinine," suggested Dick. "That's all we could do if our neighbors lived next door."

"Why, there's no house out there," said Aunt Jule. "I'd like to know where you're going to live. I s'pose you'll argue that you don't need a house. Or are Dick and Phil intending to put up a bungalow for you?"

Dick bristled, but Becky pretended not to notice the sarcasm. Phil, at ten, could not be of much assistance at bungalow building.

"Uncle Jim said that we could live in the new barn. That's a good-sized building, and it's partitioned off into three rooms. At first he only intended to have us live there while the house was being built, but after he was sick he said we'd better not plan for the house at all. There wouldn't be enough left to build it, after we paid the bills for his sickness, and besides, we might not want to stay out there after our homesteading was over. He said the best Child in the world started out in a barn and it wouldn't hurt us to live there fourteen months."

"And where will you keep the stock if you use their stalls for your parlor?" asked her aunt disagreeably.

"We're only going to have a cow and two horses. Uncle Jim had already bought the team or we wouldn't need two. We may sell one when we get through hauling. He said that we could keep them in the shack that he had intended for a tool shed."

"I suppose you're going to farm, too?"

"Now, Aunt Jule, you know we can't farm; Uncle Jim didn't have any idea of our doing it

after — after he was sick," said Dick, his face
red with the combined effort of tack-pulling and
temper-holding. "He said that we were to have
only ten acres broken and planted to corn for
the stock. We're going to put in a garden, ourselves, so that with our vegetables and our milk
and our eggs we can get along. We can plant
a garden and take care of the chickens and the
animals. But we're no farmers."

"You're right about that," said Aunt Jule, in
a tone that was as aggravating as it was intended
to be. "No farmers, and not much gardeners,
either, unless the Dakota air gives you new energy. Becky's a pretty fair hand for work, but
it'll be a new thing for you, young man. Hoeing
potatoes ain't as entertaining as track-teaming,
you'll find. And how are you going to pay for
all the things you'll need, out there? You'll find
you're not millionaires, when the will's read."

Becky tried, for Uncle Jim's sake, to keep resentment out of her voice. "We shan't have to
wait for a will to learn that. He always told us
about his affairs, and we know exactly what we'll
have to live on. You see, Aunt Jule, he had

everything — almost everything — bought and paid for last winter, for we expected to be out there early this spring. We'll start out with enough to carry us until our first crop is due."

"Easy come; easy go. You've never had any experience at handling money. What you going to count on for income if your crop fails?"

"We'll have the rent from this house."

"I s'pose you think twenty-five dollars a month would keep you."

"It may have to."

"Well, it's a fool idea, all the way round. Of course I haven't anything to say about it unless I'm appointed guardian, and I don't suppose Jim ever looked ahead far enough to plan for that. I never was one to put my oar in, anyway. You children would be far better off if you stayed right here in Platteville. Becky's all ready for normal school, and in three years she'd have her certificate and be ready to teach. Then she could support the rest of the family while Dick is preparing. Your uncle didn't have any too much to leave you, anyway. You'd better not spend the last cent of it on a wild-goose chase like this."

"But where could we live?" said Becky. "This house is rented to the Glovers. We'd have to find a home, and we haven't enough money to live and go to school and to pay rent, too. And we'd have to give up that land. Uncle Jim had already filed on it, he'd built the barn and the shack, and he paid for the stock this spring. A lot of our goods are already out there. No, we've gone too far to back out now. Uncle Jim thought it was best to go ahead. And besides, Aunt Jule, now that he's — gone, I just feel as though I *can't* stay on without him." She pulled at a bent and rusty tack with unseeing eyes.

"Nonsense," said Aunt Jule. "You can't give up to any such feeling as that. Death comes to everybody in this world, sooner or later. I was prostrated when I lost Sam, but where would I be if I had given in to my grief? And he was a husband, not an uncle. You've all got to brace up, just as I did."

Dick rubbed his coat sleeve across his eyes. "We *are* bracing up," he said fiercely.

Aunt Jule settled back in her rocker. "Well, I s'pose there's no use trying to tell you anything if your uncle's got your affairs all settled. You won't starve during the summer — you'll probably have enough money to carry you for awhile. But you'll be back as soon as cold'weather starts, and I'll be expected to take the four of you in."

Becky shook her head.

"You needn't worry; we'd never come to you," exclaimed Dick.

"You may be glad to come, yet. I've heard those Dakota stories before. No homesteader is ever able to keep the land he settles; it always goes back to the bank that has loaned him money. And four children! How are *you* going to run a farm? Why, you're not even old enough yet to keep from fighting among yourselves!"

It was impossible to deny this, much as they longed to do it. Neither meekness nor tolerance were characteristics of the Linvilles. Becky ignored the accusation, but she answered with spirit: "We don't intend to 'run a farm.' Uncle Jim had no idea of our doing that. What we expected to do was to hold down that claim for fourteen months till we got the title to the land. And we're going to do it."

"Fourteen months is fourteen months," remarked Aunt Jule, impersonally. "There'll be no grocery store to run to for canned peas, and wood and water won't carry themselves."

Over her candlestick Becky gave Dick a wink. It was a wink of large proportions, signifying caution, self-restraint, and a third element which Dick well understood. Being interpreted it meant "The less you say the less chance she gets." And knowing the truth of that hint, the boy held his tongue as well as his temper. It was Becky who said slowly:

"We know that it's going to be hard living, Aunt Jule; Uncle Jim told us the bad things as well as the good. But he had everything planned for us, and we're going to do the best we can. If it were twice as hard living as he told us we'd still go, because he wanted it. I can go to normal school after we prove up, but it's the proving up we're going to do first."

Aunt Julia's sharp little eyes swept over the room, taking note of all the gaps. "So that's why you've been moving out things, right along. I believe you gave me to understand that you were house-cleaning."

"That was I ; not Beck," said her nephew, without a show of repentance. "I didn't tell you a lie, either. You asked me if we were house-cleaning, and I told you that it was house-cleaning *time*. It is, isn't it?"

Aunt Julia ignored him. "You going to take all the furniture, Becky?"

"Part of it. Uncle Jim had everything that we would want listed, and most of it has already gone out. We're going to pack the few last things we'll need. The rest we'll store or sell."

Aunt Jule made a noise with her tongue that sounded like "tchick, tchick." "Well, it's a pretty poor notion, to my way of thinking. However, I wasn't asked for my opinion, and I don't intend to give it. You going to have enough money to carry you?"

"We're going to have enough to make our first payment on the land, to pay for our breaking, and what supplies we'll need this summer. Uncle Jim had canned goods and claim clothes bought for a year, and he said we wouldn't need much else. The horses and wagon and the cow are paid for. Even the chickens are ordered.

He thought of everything. But of course we've got to help ourselves."

"I'm surprised that your uncle was that practical. It's the wild life out there that took his fancy — not the farming. He was always crazy about out-of-door things. I think that's what gave him his stroke — the continual tramping around with you kids. He never had any sense about taking care of himself."

"He never thought about himself; always about us," said Becky. She faced the wall to hide the tears that would rise.

"He sure was dippy about wild things," agreed Dick. "He said when he got to Dakota he was going to breathe for the first time since he left the sea. It took a hundred and sixty acres of open land, he said, to give a man a real breath of air." The boy pulled out a tack with a strong dig of his screw-driver. "There, that's the last. We're clear around, Beck."

His aunt rose from her chair. "I s'pose I might as well move into the sitting-room if you're going to roll that linoleum. I can talk just as well through the door."

Even through her tears Becky smiled at Dick's glance. Aunt Jule never had any difficulty in making speech, anywhere.

Their aunt settled herself in the doorway. "I was surprised, this afternoon, when I didn't see you in the black veil I sent over to you. He was only your uncle, but he's been a real father to you, and that blue hat of yours was too gay for a funeral."

"It was what he wanted, Aunt Julia. He said he hoped to goodness we wouldn't *see* black every time we thought of him."

Dick broke the bonds of hospitality, at last. "Uncle Jim hated mourning clothes. He used to say it was easier to put on black after folks were gone than to treat them white while they were here. He *told* Beck to shy if you tried to put a mourning net on her, Aunt Jule."

His aunt pushed back the chair from the doorway. "Well, I see there's no advising you children. I try to do my best for you because I can't forget that your mother was Sam's own sister, but you're set in your own way, just as she and Jim always were. You'll have to try out the

Dakota idea for yourself. Only don't come crying back to me when your money's all gone, and you want a home."

Dick rolled the linoleum over so fiercely that he almost caught her feet in it. "We won't! we won't!" he exclaimed. "We'd hate living with you just as much as you'd hate having us."

"You needn't snap at me that way," said Aunt Jule. "Even your Uncle Jim wouldn't approve of your being so sassy. I guess I'll be getting along before you roll my shoes in with your oilcloth." She raised herself stiffly from her seat. "I s'pose you're not thinking of taking that big red chair with you, are you? That would be hard to pack. I'll be glad to keep it for you if you want to store it; it's the most comfortable chair you have."

"We're going to crate it and send it out to Dakota."

"Well, it's yours; take it if you want. When are you going?"

"Next Saturday. We've got to be out of the house by that time, for the Glovers want to move in Monday. There isn't so much left for us to do; we were almost packed when Uncle Jim was taken sick. I suppose our goods are already in Dakota."

"Piling up freight charges," commented Aunt Jule cheerily. "Well, I think I'll be going on; my advice doesn't seem to be worth anything to either of you. School's about out, anyway, and I don't suppose one summer of homesteading is going to hurt you. Only when you come back in the fall with everything spent, don't say I didn't warn you." She pulled her black cape around her shoulders, and stepped over the roll of linoleum.

"We won't," promised Dick.

The kitchen door closed behind Aunt Jule. Then it opened again, wide enough to admit her face. "Have you thought of rattlesnakes?" she asked. Then she shut the door and walked briskly down the gravel walk.

Brother and sister faced each other in the kitchen. "Can you beat *that?*" demanded Dick. "Our most comfortable chair; therefore leave it with her."

"I don't mind the chair," said Becky. "But I

can't stand it when she begins on Uncle Jim —
darling Uncle Jim, who never had a word of hate
for anyone in the world, even his crank of a sister-
in-law."

"Well, there's one good thing about Aunt Jule:
she makes you so mad at her that you forget everything else — even his dying. And I'm glad not
to think about that, even for a minute."

Becky was laying newspaper and burlap down
on the floor. "We might as well finish this up
tonight," she said. "That will leave the last
crating for tomorrow. Thursday we'll pack the
trunks; Friday we'll store the beds and sleep at
the Dennisons' and Saturday — " She did not
finish the sentence.

THEIR first real knowing of Uncle Jim had come
eight years before. Dick's earliest memory of
him had been of a pair of arms, with a blue anchor
tattooed on one of the wrists, holding him up to
kiss his father's dead face. And Becky, who had
been nine, remembered the stream of tears that
had flowed down her mother's face as Uncle Jim
had said: "You're all going back with me. Now

I can have what I've always wanted — a home." He had sold their little house in Trenton, packed their household goods, and brought the whole family, carrying the two babies himself, back to the old home in Platteville. "I'm tired of the sea," he said. "I'll be glad to settle down." It was years before Becky stopped believing that, and realized that making the home was not wholly a favor to Uncle Jim. For the first four years he had been father to the little family; after that his duties were doubled, for he had to be mother as well. Becky was thirteen when Mrs. Linville died, and she could still remember her uncle's: "It's up to you and me now, Becky. If you'll do the home-making I'll do the cooking and the spanking." No one but Uncle Jim could have made her smile, then.

And so the Linville home went on. Aunt Jule shook her head over the way "Mary's children were being raised," and said it was the craziest house she had ever seen. Uncle Jim's house-keeping was done by a process of elimination. His sailor's training had given him a hatred for uncleanliness or disorder, but it had also taught

him what was necessary and what unnecessary
for living. Of books, fresh air, games, music,
light, and food the house was full; of ornaments
and draperies, and what Uncle Jim called "gimcracks" there were none. Before and after his
business hours Becky and he had fought out the
cooking together; he had given the two older
children their first lessons in darning. He had
enforced a system of co-operation, of order, and
of waiting upon themselves. He had let them
fill the house with playfellows and gayety and
noise, but he had no patience with laziness or
selfishness or fine airs. As a house Uncle Jim's
establishment may not have been a perfect success; as a home it was a triumph.

Two years before, when the Rosebud Indian
Reservation was thrown open for settlement, Uncle Jim had gone out to file on the land. He had
not been one of the fortunates who drew claims,
but he came back in love with the country and
enthusiastic about its future. "I don't believe
I'd ever be lonely for salt water, out there," he
confided to Becky. "Those prairies are seas
made out of grass."

In the fall following, when all of the land not already filed upon was thrown open to squatters, he went out again. He found a quarter-section which had been left tenantless because of a stony hill that was included within its limits. True, the hill occupied ten acres of the three hundred and sixty, but the soil was a rich, sandy loam, all of the land except that hill was fit for cultivation, and a little creek, winding its way through the level meadow, would be a fine thing for stock. He filed on the claim, "established residence" by putting up a good-sized barn and a smaller shack, and after a month of work had come home to the children full of enthusiasm. All winter they had planned and purchased and packed, intending to start for the new home in the early spring. And then, the week before they were ready to leave, with almost all their household goods sent on before them, a clot of blood in Uncle Jim's brain had halted everything. Gradually movement and speech came back to the stricken man, but strength had evidently gone to stay. All his thought during those last weeks of his life had been of the children and their new home. His love and his will dominated the nerveless hands and the feeble brain. He compelled himself to live long enough to plan their fourteen months of homesteading for them. Then he died.

Becky's thoughts went back over that last year as she rolled the papers about the linoleum. The homesteading had seemed a lark and an adventure with Uncle Jim there to direct, to decide, and to superintend. But now it was a leap into the dark, a trip on an uncharted sea without a pilot. Could she hold the crew together, and steer the boat? Dared she start out on that unknown sea, with no compass but Uncle Jim's notebook, no rudder but the memory of his words? She dared not try it. And yet she must go.

"Dick," she said softly. She hesitated, and tucked in the ends of the newspapers as she felt for the right words.

"Speak up," encouraged Dick. "What's eating you?"

Becky dropped back upon her knees. "I'm scared to death to start off."

"Aunt Jule's done that to you — the old crape-hanger."

"No, it isn't Aunt Jule; it's I. I'm not sure that I'm going to be able to put it across. I'm not afraid of snakes or blizzards or hard work, but I'm panicky about myself. Maybe I'm not going to be big enough to do it if I don't have Uncle Jim."

"You'll not be doing it alone; you'll have us."

"The kids will help, of course, but they aren't old enough to take any responsibility. It's the responsibility I dread."

"You won't have to take all of it, Dumb-bell. I'm going to hold up my end, ain't I?"

"I know you will, Dick; I'm sure of that. But it isn't just the work and the planning! it's the keeping together. I don't know if we can do that. We've got to stand against everybody else, just as Uncle Jim said. Oh, Dick, we *mustn't* fight!" She laid a dusty hand on his grimy overalls.

"Well, I won't fight if you treat me right," said her brother gruffly. He was boy enough to wriggle away from her caress, but man enough to understand what that caress meant. "Uncle Jim told me what he wanted me to do, and I'm going to do it," he said, in a brusque voice. "We'll work it out, some way, Beck. Hold those papers down, and let me do the rolling."

A small, white-robed figure stood in the doorway, a sharp-chinned little girl, with a freckled nose, and gray-green eyes. "Aunt Jule gone?" she asked.

"Look in the most comfortable seat; if she's not there she isn't here," said Dick.

"Did you tell her that she could have the red chair?"

"Neither the red chair, nor you and Phil. I think with a little urging she would have kept all three of you," teased her brother.

"She wouldn't keep me," said Joan. "I never would stay in her horrible house." And she shivered.

"You'd better run back to bed," said Becky. "Don't you dare take cold before Saturday."

"I can't sleep. I just get about there, and then I think of him again."

Becky smiled at her through tears. "Remember what he told you, Joan."

"I do," said the little girl, "But sometimes I can't."

"Come on up," said Becky.   "I'll tuck you in." She squeezed the thin little hand as the two went back upstairs together.

Dick wrapped burlap over the long roll of linoleum, and tied each end with rope.   A new, queer sensation seemed to hang about a spot somewhere between his heart and his throat — a feeling that he would fasten up the old part of his life when he turned the key in the door.   School days, track team, baseball nine, the skating rink, old friends, would be left behind when he went. Would there be something to take their place in that new country that Uncle Jim loved so well? He stood a moment, looking around the dismantled room — at the bright spot on the wall that the kitchen clock had covered, the pencil lines on the doorway, where Uncle Jim had measured heights on each birthday, the empty table drawer with a single knife left in it, the mark that Uncle Jim's rubber heel had made when the pantry floor was newly varnished.

Then he got out pen and ink and wrote a tag, which he fastened with wire to the roll of linoleum.   It was addressed to

Richard Linville

Dallas

Tripp County   *South Dakota*

CHAPTER II

THE JUMPING-OFF PLACE

GOOD–BY, Mary, you blessed old thing!"
"Good-by, Becky dear. Good luck.
Come back soon."

It seemed as though everybody in Platteville
were at the Northwestern Station on Saturday
afternoon. Old, young, and middle-aged stood
on the platform, while parcels and boxes were
passed through the window with the affectionate
good-bys. The farewell was too much for
Becky, and as the train pulled away from the

mass of waving handkerchiefs, she sank back into the seat with tears in her eyes. "The dear, dear people!" she said.

"They gave us a fine send-off," said Dick, speaking gruffly to hide a shake in his voice.

Becky shaded her eyes to look back at the little town set in its nest of green. As the train crossed the Rountree Branch on the trestle she looked up the valley to the graveyard where they had left Uncle Jim. Between her heart and her throat was a leaden weight that both pressed and choked. It seemed as though she must stop that train, clamber down the steps and run up the hillside to tell Uncle Jim that she couldn't go.

"When do we eat?" inquired Phil.

Joan said nothing. She settled herself back into the red plush with delight written all over her expressive little face. Her last trip on the railroad had been made at the age of three months, and she had never dreamed of the splendors of velvet and veneer that lay behind the windows of a chair car. What joy to be going on a real trip, amid such luxury! She was oblivious to the dust on the seats, the cinders on the window-sills, the faint odor of lunch boxes that pervaded the car. She gave a bounce of ecstasy on the hard, plush seat. "Just like a throne!" she said to herself.

At Ipswich Phil made a trip to the water-cooler, being parched with thirst after four miles of travel, and it was during his absence that the news agent passed by Joan. A very friendly man, with much gold in his teeth and on his cap, who called her "sister," and laid on the seat beside her a package of gum, a fortune-telling ring, and a bottle made of parafine, with a delicious-looking red liquid inside. He passed on without waiting for her grateful "Oh, thank you!"

Joan quickly concealed both bottle and ring. No use in exhibiting her treasures all at once; it would prolong the pleasure to produce them one at a time. Moreover, they wouldn't have to be shared so generously. But she opened the package of gum, took out a thin wedge of Yucatan for Phil and a mint stick for herself; then put the rest away. When Phil came back her jaws were busy. She produced his stick.

"Where'd you get it?"

"None of your beeswax," answered his sister.

Phil amicably accepted the dainty. "Of course you'd annex the spearmint for yourself," he said. "Lookit, Jonie, quick. Ain't that a swell cave up there in those rocks? If I find one like that in Dakota I'm going to fix it up and live in it. Betcha there'd be bears in a cave like that."

"Uncle Jim said there weren't any bears in South Dakota."

"Well, there may be now, since all the settlers have come in. Bears always go where there's good eating."

Joan shivered happily. It was a terrifying thought — one that she feared, yet found delicious to harbor.

"It would be a swell place for wolves, too," said Dick.

"They don't have wolves; only coyotes."

"Ain't those wolves, I'd like to know?"

The door slammed, and the news agent came back through the car again. He guided his swinging tray of wares between the seats till he stopped in front of Joan, and gave a swift glance over her lap.   "Well, sister, how were they?"

"Oh, fine!"

"Thirty-five cents," said the news agent.

"Sir?"   She must have misunderstood him.

"Thirty-five cents.   Ten for the gum, ten for the cordial and fifteen for the ring."

Joan turned very red.   "I thought you gave them to me."

The news agent showed the gold in his teeth, but his smile seemed, somehow, less pleasant. "What do you think I'm in business *for?"*

Joan cast a quick look across the car.   Becky and Dick, with their backs turned, were looking out of the window.   She produced a ten-cent piece from the little bead bag in her lap, and the ring and the bottle from her pocket.   How she hated them both, now!

The agent looked at them with scorn.   "I can't sell those things after they've been bumping around in your pocket."

"Do you mean you won't take 'em back?"

"I sure won't."

Joan's face was despairing. She flushed till even the freckles on her nose were invisible. "But I haven't got any more money."

"I can't stand here gassing all day over thirty-five cents," said the news agent. "Where's yer folks?"

Phil stood up in his seat, and shook down his clothes. There was a little jingle. From his hip pocket he took out two nickels. From his blouse waist he extracted, one by one, five pennies. "Here's a quarter," he said to the man in uniform. You can take back the ring; she never damaged *that* package."

The man looked disagreeable, but he picked up the money and the goods, and started away.

"Hey," said Phil. "That bottle belongs to *us*. We paid for that."

The news agent tossed the parafine bottle toward them, as he started away.

"You're a good boy, Phil Linville," said his sister gratefully. "That was the money you got for your rabbit."

"You got to make it up to me, some way. Anyway, I guess there are plenty of rabbits where we're going. C'mon, Jonie, I'll let you drink the juice, an' I'll chew the parafine. Don't let Beck see you; she'll say we'll spoil our meal." And thus reminding himself, he crossed the aisle and touched his elder sister's shoulder. "Becky," he said, "When are we going to eat?"

THEY ate their luncheon in the park in Galena, sitting under the shade of the hard maples. Then they climbed the steep hill that led to General Grant's old home. It was after visiting hours, but the caretaker, moved by Becky's almost reverent questions, unlocked the door and showed them through the old-fashioned rooms.

"Is she the Grants' aunt?" whispered Joan, with her hand on Becky's dress.

"Why?"

" 'Cause she calls 'em all by their first names — Fred and Jesse and Julia."

The caretaker heard the question, and smiled. "Don't wonder you ask that," she said, goodnaturedly. "You know, living here in the house, and talking about them to people, the way I do, every day, you get so you feel as though they were your own folks. Nellie has great-grandchildren now, but I always think of her as a pretty little girl, looking into the mirror in that small room upstairs. And the General — why, I never go up the front steps that I don't look for him sitting in that porch chair, with his cigar in his mouth."

Joan was enraptured with Galena, with its steep little streets running into the rocky hills above the town, the vine-covered church that was built into the solid limestone behind it, the deserted graveyard that was now a playground. "I don't see why General Grant ever went away from here," she said. "He could sleigh ride down these hills so fast that he'd go up on the other side. Then all he'd have to do would be to turn his sled around. Wish we were going to live here instead of in Dakota."

IT WAS ten o'clock at night before the Northwestern train came in, and Phil and Joan were dead with sleep when the Linvilles started on their way to Omaha. Becky, not daring the extravagance of a sleeper, made them as comfortable as she could with blankets and pillows, and the two went immediately to sleep. Dick stretched himself out on the seat with his overcoat and sweater, and soon followed suit. The train clanked its way over the prairies, with only an occasional light to show that the towns were far apart and small. Becky took out the steamer rug and curled up inside of it, but sleep would not come. All that was sure and tried lay behind, in Platteville; before her stretched the unknown. She thought of the change of cars ahead of her in Omaha, of the freight that must be identified and claimed at their journey's end, of the stock that they must find, of the supplies that they must buy. How was she to do all these things as Uncle Jim would have them done? She felt inadequate for the task, too young and inexperienced to meet what the next day was sure to bring.

She reached out for her suit-case, which lay on the seat opposite, and took out a thin green book which lay near the top. The light which hung from the center of the car swung with the train's motion, and cast shadows over the handwriting on the pages. It was the note-book which Uncle Jim had made for them in the last days of his illness. She turned the leaves till she came to:

OMAHA

Arrive 8 :00 A.M. *Illinois Central. Leave* 8 :45 A.M. *on Northwestern.*

N.W. train goes out at the same station. Eat a hot breakfast at the depot. Buy lunch for the next two meals. Don't hurry. You have plenty of time.

This is the home stretch. You'll love the prairie.

DALLAS

Arrive 8 :00 P.M., *and go to hotel three blocks up Main Street. In early morning buy your last supplies. Inquire at the Star Lumber Yard for the superintendent, Mr. Cleaver. He'll tell you where our freight is stored and will see that the team and the wagon are brought over to meet you. Depend on what he tells you; he is the cream of Tripp County.*

Get a man to help load the boxes on to the wagon. Start with box number 1, *and don't take more than the horses can carry. Dick will have to come back for the rest, later.*

*The bay horse is lazier than his partner; see that
he takes his share of the pull.*

*19 miles straight north to the claim.   Get a man
to drive with you and help unload.   Look for
the prairie dog town as you drive past the hill
with the watermark.*

Play fair, everybody, and all help.

*If you don't like the prairie then I've counted
wrong.*

The dearness of Uncle Jim!   Becky could almost hear his laughing voice in the words.   He
seemed so near, so *with* her as she read his in-
structions.   The worry stopped.   Things were
not so scary after all.   She pushed the little book
up under her pillow, turned her back to the light,
and went off to sleep.

AFTER they left Omaha the world began to
change.   It was opener country; the sky reached
farther; the towns grew fewer.   The men who
boarded the train had wide-brimmed hats, and
many of them wore red handkerchiefs about their
necks.   At Niobrara a party of Indians got on —
the younger ones in store clothes, the father and

mother in moccasins, flannel shirt and blanket shawl. At Norfolk the Linville children got off the car for a moment to stretch their tired legs, and there they met the prairie wind that Uncle Jim had described — the unceasing, never-waning breeze that tore at their clothes and zoomed in their ears; that attacked, rather than caressed. They were glad to get on the train again.

The occasional towns were only single streets of false-fronted stores with a few frame houses. The trees were rare wind-breaks. Finally both town and streets vanished in a sea of green grass that ran into the sky.

The west burned with a great fire. The sun turned into a molten ball of red gold. Phil began to rummage in the lunch box, but Joan, with her freckled face against the car window, watched the ball drop down behind the world. The skies turned from red to orange, from orange to purple, from purple to gray. The porter lit the lamp in the center of the car. Joan yielded her little frame to the swaying train. "Clink, clank" she sang to the accompaniment of the banging metal beneath her. Then she took out her block of paper, produced a much-chewed pencil and wrote:

> *Clink, clank, clink, clank,*
> *The sun is setting behind the banck.*
> *Ime going out to live on a clame*
> *Where raseing mellons is our ame.*

IT WAS evening when they pulled into Dallas. And there a little, flat town lay between the prairie behind them and the prairie ahead of them, with the two shining railway tracks ending in waving grass. Aunt Jule had been right about one thing: it *was* the Jumping-off Place.

"We can't bother Mr. Cleaver tonight," decided Becky. "We'll go to the hotel, get to bed, and make an early start in the morning."

The children made their way up the long street — the only street of the town. When Becky found the stores open she decided that they might save time by buying their supplies at night. So while the two children sat in the hotel, looking with interest at the moccasined Indians and the occasional cowboys that passed, Dick and Becky made their list and did their shopping.

"Ye gods," said Dick as he jingled the two solitary dimes that were left from his twenty dollar bill, "How that money hopped off!"

Becky looked worried. "It did go fast. But everything we bought was a necessity."

"Except that cloth you ordered. No use for that on a claim."

"I bought three yards of cretonne! And those cartridges of yours cost a dollar and a half."

"Don't shake your gory locks at me! Those cartridges will give you fresh game to cook."

Becky's eyes snapped. "To cook for whom?"

"Thought you were going to can the scrapping?"

The girl looked ashamed. "I am. We mustn't, Dick."

"See that you don't, then."

Becky changed the subject. "I'm glad that's the last of the spending. We ought not to need anything else but oil for months."

"*Ought not!* We *can't!*" Dick had had his first awakening to the slippery quality of money.

THE children were awake early next morning. At the lumber yard they inquired for the superintendent, and a chubby-faced man that looked like Santa Claus came out of the office at once. He shook hands all around with a heartiness that was a real welcome. "So you're the young Linvilles," he said. "I've heard enough about you so I know you all. I was afraid you'd given up the homesteading idea until I had that letter from your uncle three weeks ago. Is he going to be able to make the trip out, later?"

"Uncle Jim died last week," said Becky.

The man saw the quick tears that sprang to four pairs of eyes. "I was afraid of that," he said. "He wrote me that his mortgage on life was just about due, but I hoped he was mistaken. His assets, he said, he was going to send out here. And you're the assets, I take it."

"Yes, sir," said Dick, not quite understanding.

"Well, I suppose we'd better start your homesteading proposition, right away," said Mr. Cleaver, briskly. "You're a bit late, anyway, and we can't afford to waste any time. Wait till I get my hat, and we'll go and see about your supplies. Lucky thing your new team happens to be in town today. I saw it here less than an hour ago."

"We bought all our supplies," said Becky.

"When?"

"Last night, after the train got in."

"How did you know what to buy?"

"Uncle Jim made out the list for us. Dick and I went together."

"Aren't you pretty young kids to be handling your own cash?"

"I've done the marketing ever since I was fourteen."

Mr. Cleaver glanced at the resolute mouth, at the steady blue eyes, at the decided young chin. "You kids have the 'git up and git,'" he said, with admiration in his voice. "You'll do."

There was admiration in his face, too, as he watched the goods being loaded. With cap off, sleeves rolled up and flannel shirt open at the throat, Dick fell upon the freight. Becky and the two youngest children joined in the carrying, while Dick and a man from the lumber yard lifted the heavier boxes. Mr. Cleaver went back

and forth on various errands, but returned each
time to find the work going on steadily.   There
was no disagreement, no waste of steps, no false
moves.   The four children moved like clock-
work, and in less than an hour the Linville wagon
was loaded and ready to start.

"Why not get all your goods out at once?" suggested Mr. Cleaver.   "Wubber, a homesteader
who lives a mile from your place, is in Dallas,
and going right past your claim.   If he has room
on his wagon for the rest of your things you'd save
time and it wouldn't cost you any more than to
make the extra trip yourselves."

Becky and Dick eagerly agreed to the plan.
A boy was sent out for Mr. Wubber, a blond man
whose face was so sunburned that he seemed to
have the wrong wig on.   When he learned where
the new homesteaders were to settle he refused to
accept pay for the use of his team.

"You give me my noon meal, and we'll call it
square.   My wife would give me tittery eye if
I took pay fer hauling from a near neighbor."

Joan and Phil looked at each other.   What
was tittery eye?

"How near?" asked Dick. "I thought you lived a mile from us."

"That's close neighbors in Tripp County," said Mr. Wubber.

"Now," said Mr. Cleaver, when the last crate had been loaded on to the wagons, "you boys had better start on. It'll take you several hours, with those loads. I'm going to take Miss Becky and the small fry out with me in my car. They'll be ready and waiting when you come. Wubber, you'll stay and help unload the kids, won't you?"

"Sure. I'll stay till they're moved in," replied Mr. Wubber. He winked one eye, which dropped a strangely white lid down on his sunburned face. "This is wash day at our house, and there ain't much to come home *to* on wash days."

"I druther go out on the wagon," said Phil.

"Nothing doing," put in Dick, decidedly. "You're going just as you're told."

"You're not the boss of me."

Becky broke in quickly. "The horses have enough load as it is, Phil. Besides, you'll get a chance to look around at the place before Dick comes and we'll all have to get to work. It's a wonderful chance to drive out with Mr. Cleaver."

Mr. Cleaver cast an amused glance at the girl. "You know how to manage 'em, don't you? I was going out your way, anyway, Phil, and I'd like to show you the country as we go. It'll give me company on my drive, and you a chance to look over your land. I've got to stop at the house a moment before I'm ready, but I shan't keep you waiting long."

He piled the children into his car and drove up Main Street to a gray bungalow, which had a real porch and the only awnings in town. When he came out of the house, fifteen minutes later, he carried a basket which he put between the two seats. "All set," he said. "Let's start."

At the edge of the town the prairie seemed to roll in upon them. Becky looked out upon a world of vivid green and blue. A sea of grass, soft, lush, deep, rose around them, swept by waves of wind that made silver billows through the sea. Miles of this green stretched before them. It was a world of grass — no trees, no rocks, no land-marks of any kind. Only the gray trail that ran through the prairie, and now and then a tiny shack, built of boards, or a house made of sod.

Joan gazed over the miles of grass with a wistful expression on her sharp little face. "Aren't there any *things* on the prairie?" she asked. "Is it all just grass?"

Mr. Cleaver laughed — a deep-sounding chuckle that seemed to come from his waist, rather than his throat. "That's the way it seems to everyone at first. But wait awhile, and you won't find it as bare as you think."

"What'll we find?"

"All the flowers that grow. Chipmunks and prairie dogs and coyotes and muskrats and beavers, and turtles almost big enough for you to ride, and now and then a wolf —— "

"There, I told you!" interrupted Phil.

"And meadow-larks, and quail that go drumming about in the springtime. Wild geese and prairie chickens and big black hawks. Indian arrow-heads in the earth and Indian water-marks on the hills. Wild plum thickets and ground cherries. And the most wonderful sunsets you ever saw."

"Gee!" said Phil. His sigh of ecstasy was for plums, not sunsets.

The car sped along the trail that looped and doubled upon itself like a ribbon. It rounded bottom-land that was almost swampy, where the grass grew long and showed its silver side when the wind blew across it. In the deep, vivid green was a riot of color — the blue of the liverwort, the yellow of swamp buttercup, and here and there a late red lily that looked like a stain of blood in the grass. Over it swung red-winged black-birds, and from its depths meadow-larks called their six liquid notes.

Mr. Cleaver glanced down at Becky's face. "How do you like it?"

The girl's eyes were alight. "Oh, wonderful! If Uncle Jim could just see it!"

"You're going to be all right if it strikes you that way, at first," said Mr. Cleaver. "As for your uncle seeing it, he did. I drove him over this very trail, just about a year ago."

"Didn't he say he liked it?"

"Over and over. He was just crazy about the country; said that he didn't know land could be so much like the sea."

"How did *you* come to bring him out?"

"Well, I happened to meet him the first day he landed in Dallas. He was the kind of man that would make a dent in your memory — he was so unusual a fellow — and we took a shine to each other right away. When he failed to get any land in the drawing I was as disappointed as he was. I told him not to give up his idea of coming out here; that I'd keep my eye open for a claim before squatting time. It was I who wrote him that this land was to be thrown open, and when he came out to take a look at it I drove him over here."

"Do you take that much trouble for all homesteaders?"

"Not by any manner of means. But your uncle was the kind of citizen we need. And if we can't get him we're glad to have his proxies."

"We're pretty poor substitutes for Uncle Jim."

"I'm not so sure about that," said Mr. Cleaver. "When I first got his letter telling me he was de-

pending on you to do the homesteading, I wrote
back discouraging the idea. I told him that I
didn't think it a practical thing for four kids to
undertake claim living; you wouldn't last out the
summer. I had a letter from him four days later
in the shaky handwriting that came after his illness. It was just six words long: 'Wait till you
see the kids.' And since I have seen you and that
brother of yours take hold this morning, I guess
that your uncle was right."

Becky's eyes softened at the praise. She
dared not trust her voice to reply.

"Too bad his sickness put you back so far.
You're three months later than you should be.
But you're lucky in having this a backward year;
even the people who had their crops in early this
spring aren't seeing much results."

"We're not going to have any crops but sod
corn," said Becky. "We're going to garden, not
farm. Uncle Jim said it wasn't too late for potatoes. And I'm bringing two big boxes of
plants. I set out tomatoes and cabbage, and every
other vegetable that I dared transplant, in boxes,
weeks ago. Uncle Jim had the ground plowed

and disked and harrowed last October. We ought to get *some* results."

"Yes, he worked like a Trojan in those weeks that he was here last fall. He must have done a lot of the building himself, for the carpenter who worked for him was a poor sort of wood butcher. Your uncle came in for more lumber one day when I was rushed with work. My two helpers were gone, and I'd been filling orders, answering telephone and rustling lumber, myself. 'How goes it?' he asked, as I scurried around to find a man to help him fill his wagon. 'Too much work to suit me,' I said, 'I'm sick and tired of keeping my nose to the grindstone.' I remember how hot he looked, as he stopped in his loading. 'Well,' he said, 'I don't feel that way about work. If the Lord will supply the grindstone, I'll furnish the nose.' I never forgot that."

Becky smiled through her tears. She could almost hear Uncle Jim saying it.

The car went over a hill, and two deep blue peaks showed, outlined against a lighter blue sky. "You're on the home stretch now," said Mr. Cleaver. "Those are the Dog Ear Buttes, twelve miles away from your claim. You'll look at them every day for the next five years — or are you planning the five-year residence?"

"No, only fourteen months. Uncle Jim said we never could raise enough on the place to feed Phil five years."

"Proving up will be over almost before you start. Here, look down through the valley; you can get a peek at your new home."

The children "peeked." The trail curved down a gentle incline, then around three buildings that stood outlined against the western sky. A square of gray ground about them, where the sub-soil had been thrown up and trampled down, made a patch in the green prairie grass. As they came nearer they saw a thin fringe of shrubbery that outlined, here and there, a curly little stream. The children bounced about excitedly on the back seat. "The creek! the creek!" they yelled.

"And there's the barn," said Becky.

"Don't le's call it a barn," pleaded Joan. "It's going to be our house. Le's call the shack the barn."

Mr. Cleaver drove up to the end of the barn-that-was-to-be-a-house. It was built in the shelter of a hill, so that on the north it would be cut off from the worst of the storm winds. On the south the tangled skeins of the creek emptied into a small pond. Near the back door was the well; over it a large pump.

The children jumped from the car before it had quite stopped, and ran to the end of the barn where a front door had been cut. Becky unlocked it, and they stepped inside. The building had been divided into three rooms by partitions that went part way to the ceiling. A window in each room let in light and air, and a back door, directly opposite the front, had a glass inset. The interior was unfinished. The beams ran to the roof tree, and the rafters stretched overhead, but the lumber had been planed, and was smooth, soft pine. Becky's heart sank a little. In spite of all Uncle Jim had told her, she had not expected to find things so primitive, so unprotected, and so bare.

But Mr. Cleaver seemed to feel differently. "This is fine!" he said. "You kids are going to be mighty comfortable when you get settled.

It's a palace for Tripp County. Hello, what's the matter with the window? And that one, too! Why, they're *all* broken."

Sure enough, every pane in the house was cracked, or contained fragments of glass. Broken slivers lay on the floor, and stones in the corners of the rooms explained how the damage had been done.

"The vandals!" exclaimed Mr. Cleaver. "Now who do you suppose could have done *that!*"

"It must have been someone who lives near-by," said Becky, with a troubled look. "This is such an out-of-the-way place that no one would come so far off the main road just to break windows."

"But you have no near neighbors except the Wubbers and the Courtlands. Wubber is a ne'er-do-well, but he hasn't a mean bone in his body, and the Courtlands aren't that kind at all. They're good neighbors. Probably it was some villain of a boy. Wish I could get new panes out of his hide."

"That means no windows for tonight. Lucky it isn't stormy, and that we have some mosquito bar. I suppose Dick will have to get new glass and a man to set it tomorrow. If it should rain we'd be flooded."

"I'll send a man out with the glass in the morning," offered Mr. Cleaver. "One that can set it, too. Makes me ashamed to find such miserable skunks as this in our community. We're not all like that, Miss Becky."

The girl gave him a grateful look. "I know that."

The children had wandered out into the door yard and stopped to get a drink. "This pump won't work," said Phil.

Mr. Cleaver threw the last stone through the doorway, and went out to help him. The pump handle rose and fell without resistance. "Work! of course it won't work. That pump's pulled out!" His face was wrathful. *"Look* at it! I believe someone has been trying to take it away, but couldn't quite lift it out. That's another thing that will have to be fixed, right away. You kids have got to have water."

"Is it a very expensive job?" asked Becky anxiously.

"It won't cost you a cent — not a red cent. I'll have it done myself and I'll spend the rest of my days in Dakota getting the pay from the man who did it. I'd like to have him here this minute. Fortunately, the pump isn't broken; it's just pulled loose."

"Will we dare to use the creek for drinking water?"

"You can use it for the horses. You'll have to get water at the spring, a half mile above here, for yourselves. It isn't the water I'm worrying about; it's the dirty trick. A fine welcome for you kids!"

"It would be a lot worse if you weren't here," said Becky.

"I'll do my best to help you fix things — that's all I can do now. I'll send the car out with a man, early in the morning. I ought to be getting back to Dallas; s'pose you and the children drive with me up the creek, so I can show you the spring. Maybe I can borrow a bucket for you to bring back some water."

"I think I'd better stay around here. I don't want any more windows broken, or to be gone

when Dick comes.   But I'll be glad to have Joan
and Phil go if they can find their way home
again."

"Come on, kids."   He lifted them into the car.
"Wish I could stick around and help you get settled."

"Come back and see us when we *are* settled."

"I will, and Mrs. Cleaver will come with me."
That seemed to remind him of something.   He
lifted the market basket from the car, and set it
in front of Becky.   "Don't know what my wife
would have said to me if I had brought this back
home.   She thought you might not want to stop
to cook, today.   Good-by, and good luck.   I'll
send the kids back in a few minutes."   And away
went the car and his friendly smile.

Becky opened the basket almost before they
were out of sight.   There was a loaf of home-
made bread, some thin slices of boiled ham
wrapped in waxed paper, a box of cookies, and
a jar of raspberry jam.   Her heart warmed to
the kindliness.   They were not without friends,
even in a new country.

The girl pulled up an empty nail keg, and sat

down in the doorway. It would be noon before Dick could get there; there was nothing to do but wait. She sat with hands in her lap, looking out at that intense blue of sky, that vivid green of earth, the shine and sparkle of that golden sunshine. Her eyes followed the prairie to the stake which Mr. Cleaver had pointed out as their section line. As far as eye could see that lush meadow land was theirs. Platteville, with Uncle Jim gone, was nothing to be lonely for. The Jumping-Off Place was home now.

CHAPTER III

NEIGHBORS

IT WAS nearly noon when the household goods arrived. Joan and Phil had brought back a bucket of water, explored the plum thicket, and were sending up squeals of ecstasy from the creek's edge when Mr. Wubber drove up to the door. Behind him came Dick, driving a dusty team, with a red cow switching her tail behind the loaded wagon. The two children, wild with excitement, ran to meet them.

" 'Zat our cow?" said Joan, critically. "She looks as though she had adenoids."

"All cows look that adenoidish way," remarked Phil. "May I drive her to the barn?"

"Tired?" called Becky from the doorway.

Dick wiped his dusty face. "Not tired, but dry as a cork. Got any water?"

Becky produced the pail and her pocket cup, and the two drank thirstily before they went back to the load.

"Take down the kitchen table for me," said Becky, "and the box of supplies. We'll all need lunch before we set to work."

Mr. Wubber nodded his approval. "That's the ticket!" said he.

Becky opened the cartons of groceries that they had purchased in Dallas, and set the bare table with crackers and cheese, bread and ham, and the gift cookies. She passed oranges with a generous hand. In the months to come she often looked back with a smile at her lavishness with that rarest article of prairie diet, fresh fruit.

It was not until Dick came in to lunch that he noticed the broken windows. He looked very much disturbed. "That the kind of neighbors we have around here?" he asked Mr. Wubber.

"Only one family about here that's likely to have had a hand in that. Except for them you'll find pretty fair neighbors."

"Who are they?"

"The Welps. I can't say that they did it, but it would be like 'em. The old lady isn't so bad, but her husband and the two boys are skunks."

"But why would they have it in for *us?*"

"They got it in fer everybody."

"Hope they're not *near* neighbors. Where do they live?"

Mr. Wubber looked uneasy. "Over that way," he said vaguely, with a bob of his head toward the south.

"I hope it *wasn't* neighbors," said Becky, with an anxious look. "I'd rather think it was the work of boys — mischief would be better than meanness."

"Either one lets in mosquitoes," suggested Joan.

"This is something like!" said Mr. Wubber, from his seat on a box. "Don't often get cookies like these. And the chances are I wouldn't have got much of anything this noon at home; the missus said this morning that she wasn't going to bust herself getting dinner."

Mr. Wubber was a most appreciative guest. There was nothing on the table that he didn't try, try again. Even Dick and Phil, who had no mean capacity of their own, eyed with wonder the amount consumed by their neighbor. It was not until the last crumb had vanished that he took a final mighty drink, which exhausted the water supply, and suggested that they get to work; if things had to be done you might as well git 'em out of the way.

"Better set up the oil stove first," suggested Phil. "Eating's the most important thing."

"You mustn't make an idol out of that stomach of yours, Sonny," admonished Mr. Wubber. "We better set up the beds first, soon as we get the floor spreads down."

All hands set to work. In what Joan called the middle "department," they rolled a rug down on the floor, set up a double bed, and two cots for the small children. Into that room went the only bureau, (Becky looked worried when she thought of the three drawers that must hold the family wardrobe), two chairs, and all the trunks.

"What's that corner shelf for?" asked Dick.

Becky looked at the triangular piece of painted wood that fitted into a corner of the room. Below it Uncle Jim had fastened a long rod of metal. "That's why he told us to take the clothes hangers that I was going to leave behind. He even thought of a closet for us."

Uncle Jim had evidently gone as far as he could to make the house ready for occupancy. He had built shelves and driven nails in the kitchen, painted borders around the bedroom and living-room floors, screwed hooks on the back of every door. Every sign of his thoughtfulness was a sword in Becky's wound, and the hard physical work, that somehow made her grief a little less, was a god-send. At three o'clock the beds and stove were set up, the bedding unpacked, the crates opened, and Mr. Wubber had gone. At four Dick's bed in the living-room — a bed that was to be a couch by day — was made, the mosquito netting had been tacked outside the broken windows, the oil stove had been started, and a pot of potatoes was boiling over the flame; the two rocking-chairs were in their places, and the living-room table held a reading lamp and some books. The clock and Uncle Jim's picture stood on a shelf. It began to look like home — a rough, splintery, barn-like place, but still a home.

"Now," said Becky, with a sigh of weariness and satisfaction, "That's done! My hands feel like sandpaper. Let's wash off the outer layer of dirt to limber us up a little. Then we'll have an early supper, and then we'll take a little trip around the place to see our preserves."

Dick milked the cow, the two children went to the spring for more water, and Becky fried bacon and eggs. The afternoon breeze died down. Little gold-tinged clouds began to float in the sky. The children, with less wrangling than usual, put the supper dishes back on the kitchen shelves. And the four young homesteaders, walking close together for companionship, went forth to look at their land. First down to the creek that twisted like a snake back and forth through the claim. It lay open to the sky, with no trees or brush to shade it. A little thicket of wild plums grew between it and the house — the nearest approach to a tree that was in sight.

"Gee," said Dick, "It's swell to have a creek on the place."

"We've always wanted to own some water of our own, as long as we've lived," said Becky, "and now we do."

Dick's face showed his pleasure. "I'm going to dam it up when I find the right place. No reason why we can't have a swimming hole of our own."

Phil and Joan gave a squeal of delight. "Maybe we can have swans," suggested Joan. "I'd love to have swans."

Phil eyed her with scorn. "Why don't you suggest osteriches! *I'm* going to have ducks."

"Smartie! You think you're the bossee of the place."

"Whenever you're tempted to scrap," sang Dick.

And the children joined in the gay chorus of Uncle Jim's Fight Song:

Remember your mouth is a trap . . .
As long as your teeth are set snugly and tight
You've a grip on yourself and the fellow you fight,
And the madder he gets, why the harder you bite . . .
So whenever you're having a scrap
Remember your mouth is a trap.

"Le's go over and hunt up the prairie dog town," suggested Phil. "Mr. Cleaver showed us where it is: between those two hill-ish places." He pointed to a ravine that lay ahead of them.

The young homesteaders plowed their way through the shaggy grass that grew so lush and green along the slough. They came out upon level ground where the sod had been gnawed short over an acre or so of land, and dwarf-like figures stood motionless about a yard apart. There were dozens of them, sitting up on their hind legs and looking curiously at their visitors. One by one they barked, shook their small tails, and disappeared into the holes below them as the children approached.

"No wonder they call it a town. Look at the holes, all in rows, like streets," said Joan.

"Mr. Cleaver says owls live in 'em, too," added Phil. "He said they came flying in, every afternoon, and went right down into the holes with the dogs."

"Maybe the prairie dogs have 'em for nurse girls," said Joan, down on her knees and peering into the hole nearest her. "Owls wouldn't mind being up in the night."

"Look out!" sang out Dick. He grabbed her roughly by the shoulder, pulled her up on to her feet, and to one side. Almost on the spot where she had been kneeling a dust-colored loop of horrid life uncurled and writhed away through the deep grass.

"Now you see what you've got to look out for," cried Dick. "Just luck that you didn't get bitten."

"Was that a snake?" breathed Joan, white and scared.

"It was a rattler. They always hang around prairie dogs, Uncle Jim said. I guess you've had enough for one day, Jonie. Tomorrow I'll get out the canes Uncle Jim made for us to carry when we went through tall grass. Better to scare 'em off than get a bite."

Phil looked his delight. "Oh gee, oh gee," he breathed in ecstasy. "It was as thick as my arm. I wish Clem Hayden could a' seen that: If we only had someone to show it to!"

"That," predicted Dick, "is going to be the hardest thing about homesteading. There won't be people to show things to."

They turned back to the west to find the sky ablaze. Long islands of violet cloud ran into a sea of red and orange fire. The sun was a great ball of molten gold that turned to red as they watched, and seemed to fill the entire sea. It went lower and lower in the western sky; then it sank suddenly. In a flash it was night. The frogs began to sing; along the creek tiny flashes of light began to show, now appearing, then vanishing, like shiny winks.

"What's that?" exclaimed Joan.

"Will o' the wisps," explained Becky. "It's the phosphorescence in that damp ground."

The dusk hid the rapt look on the little face at her side. Children who live with ten-year-old brothers have learned when to keep quiet, and how to avoid ridicule. Phosphorescence was a grown-up explanation; it was just as well not to dispute it. But one might have one's own thoughts. And Joan, stumbling over the dusky prairie at Becky's side, knew that she was to live for fourteen months in a wonder world, where fairy lights shone at night and fairy folk danced at the side of a creek.

"Le's climb the big hill before dark," suggested Phil.

"No," said Becky firmly. "Not tonight. We're all dead tired, and tomorrow's going to be a big day of work. Bed's the place for us."

The frogs were sending out a cracked chorus of "Jer-ro-me, Jerr-rr-rome," from the creek as they crept into their new beds. The little ones fell asleep almost as soon as they touched their pillows. Dick yawned heavily, and turned on his cot.

"Are you comfortable?" Becky called. He didn't answer, and she said nothing more.

THERE was a loud hammering on the kitchen door. Becky gave a sudden start in bed. It seemed to her that she was back in Platteville, and Uncle Jim was knocking on his bed post to ask for a drink. But the bright light was streaming through the half-way partitions, and the hot prairie sun shone through the open windows.

"I'm coming," she called, hurriedly getting into her clothes.

On the little platform that Uncle Jim had built outside of the back door stood three small children. The moment she opened the door, and saw the three tow-heads set above the burnt-brown faces, Becky knew where they belonged. "Isn't your name Wubber?" she asked.

The older girl, a child of ten, nodded a shy assent. "Ma wants to borry an east cake," she explained.

"Come in while I get it for you," said Becky. "You're the first visitors we've had. Tell me your names, so I'll know what to call you."

"I'm Crystal," said the spokeswoman. "This

here one is Venus. And the boy over there is Autumn."

The Linville children, partly dressed, peeped through the bedroom door at their guests. "Those are cow names," commented Phil.

Becky gave him a warning glance. "No cows ever had as pretty names as those. Who chose them for you?"

"Ma. She's the namer one."

"Pull in two chairs, Phil, so the children can sit down. Venus will have to sit on a box."

"We got *three* chairs to our house," said Venus.

"Have you any more children at home?"

"We got Twinkle. She's two."

Becky got out the yeast cake and handed it to the little girl, but the Wubber family showed no inclination to move. Getting breakfast in such crowded quarters was out of the question, and Becky wondered how long the visit was to last. "Suppose you children run out and play. Phil and Joan may go, too, until their breakfast's ready. Put on your overalls and look out for snakes."

"Le's go to the creek," suggested Phil.

The oldest Wubber lingered a moment at the door.

"What is it, Crystal?"

"Ma said if you seemed willing about the east cake I was to borry a tablespoon of sody, too."

The little girl took the twisted paper of soda and hurried away to join the others, just as Dick came through the doorway.

"Who are our guests?"

"The Wubbers — Crystal, Venus, and Autumn. Twinkle is at home."

Dick gazed out of the window. "They look like Huldah, Freda, and Ira. Was this a social call — east and west clasp hands?"

"Western hands clasp 'east,' " laughed Becky. "They came over for yeast cakes and soda."

"Hope they won't stay long. I want the kids to help me plant a garden. We're too late to put it off another day."

The Linville children were full of enthusiasm when they came in to breakfast. "The creek is full of tame suckers," exulted Phil.

"How can suckers be tame?"

"They *are* tame," defended Joan. "They

THE FOUR YOUNG HOMESTEADERS LOOK AT THEIR LAND

aren't scared of you at all. They come right up to you. Autumn caught four."

"Why, Joan, he had no fishing tackle."

"He didn't need any; he caught 'em in his fingers. Just put his hands down in the water at the deepest hole, and held 'em terrible still. Then when they swam by he caught 'em, just like lightning. He took 'em home for dinner; said he s'posed maybe his mother would cook 'em, if she didn't have one of her laying streaks."

"Laying streaks? What did he mean?"

"I asked him, and he said she laid around, some days. He says she ain't one for work."

"Hope you kids don't feel that way," said Dick. "We've got to start the garden, today."

Phil sighed. "I'll betcha the prairie is better to play on than to work on," he predicted.

Becky hurried through the breakfast dishes while Dick sought Uncle Jim's green book. He was silent so long that Becky called to him. "Does it tell us how to start?"

"I should say it does. Look, Beck, he's drawn the whole plan of the garden. Even marked the vegetables down, in rows for us, and has the plot measured.   No way of making a botch if we follow his directions.   Gee, doesn't this sound like him:

When you work in the garden start early and quit from noon till two o'clock.   If you get a sunstroke you won't need vegetables.
String beans are pretty safe things to pin your faith to.   Only one planting to a summer.
You're hungrier for potatoes when you're eating them than when you're planting them.
The earlier you get Becky's pieplant started the earlier she'll have rhubarb pie for you."

Becky pulled out her handkerchief to wipe her eyes.   Then she turned back to her dishes.   "I'll be out to help in a minute," she said.   "You start along, Dick."

THE sod had been turned up the fall before.   It had been plowed and harrowed and disked in the plot Uncle Jim had set apart for the garden. Even with all that work it didn't look like Wisconsin soil; it was tough of fibre, and the roots of wild roses that ran through it were like wires. It didn't seem possible to the children, remembering the powdery loam of the Platteville garden, that seeds would grow in it, but Uncle Jim must have known. They took the book out into the field, and held the corners of the leaves down with clods of earth while they planted. Turnips and carrots, tomatoes, onions, melons, and cucumbers all dropped, seed by seed, along their rows of string. Becky planned quickly prepared meals, and the children worked with unusual steadfastness and energy.

The man from Dallas drove out with new panes of glass, and not alone repaired the pump and the windows, but presented Becky with two castor bean plants which had already put out their first four leaves. "The elm trees of Dakota," he told her. They were a gift from Mr. Cleaver, he said, who had sent word that he wanted the family to have some shade to sit under. Becky planted one on either side of the door, carried a bucket full of water from the creek to water them, and sent back her grateful thanks to their new friend. "Tell him I'm going to call them Castor and Pollux" she said.

"Never heard 'em called Ann Pollacks before," said the Dallas man. "Castor beans is the Dakota name for 'em."

It was a long day, and a hot one, and when the sun went down in a burst of flaming cloud the children were tired. Becky suggested that the two small ones leave the kitchen stoop where they were helping Dick cut the seed potatoes, and go to the spring for fresh water. "The man said this morning that the well water would taste queer for a while after the pump was fixed." The children set off eagerly, and Becky took their place, cutting the eyes out of the potatoes they had brought from Wisconsin. The hard work of the past two days had taken their toll of enthusiasm, and the brother and sister talked soberly, like man and woman, as they worked.

"Pretty tired?" asked Becky.

Dick straightened up from the bushel basket. "Dead," he confessed. "I've got an ache instead of a back, tonight. I'm going to bed the moment these are done."

"I'll finish them."

"You will *not;* you haven't been exactly frittering away the day, yourself."

Becky was touched. Chivalry was a new trait in Dick, and one that she rejoiced to see. Homesteading wasn't going to be so bad if she was going to share it with someone else; it wasn't the *being* a martyr, but the feeling yourself one, that made hardship. Evidently Dick had started out with the idea he was to take his share of whatever came.

"Do you think we're going to swing it, Dick?" she asked.

Dick looked sober. "It's bigger than I thought it was going to be. Plenty of work in front of us. But some things about the place are great; guess it'll be worth while in the end. Anyway, I'm not planning to go back to Aunt Jule."

The fairy castles of golden cloud turned into masses of violet. The hush of evening began to close them in.

"It's wonderful country," said Becky, still cutting potatoes as she looked across at the blue buttes that were melting into sky. "I can hardly believe yet, that it is ours."

"In fourteen months more," exulted Dick.

A sound of hurrying feet in the grass; hurrying feet and panting breath. The children came tearing across the creek, breathless with excitement, with their pail still empty.

"Those boys — at the spring — said it was theirs — we shouldn't — set the dog on us," they cried, interrupting each other with broken snatches of sentences.

"Hey, calm down. One at a time," ordered Dick. "You tell, Phil; Joan has no breath left."

"We were up at the spring filling our pail, and two kids came along with a dog. They told us to get out of there or they'd bust our faces in. We told 'em we was only getting water, and they said it was their water, and we sure had our nerve to come and help ourselves. They were a lot biggern us and they had the dog too, so we didn't dare sass 'em back. We thought we'd fill the pail and come away, but as fast as we had it full they'd empty it. They told us we had no business up there at all; that it was their claim, and they'd been living on it for months. Finely they set the dog on us and we had to run off. They've got a shack just over the hill from the spring; we saw the roof."

"They told us to keep away from the water if we knew what was good for us," added Joan.

Dick raised his bent shoulders from the potato cutting. "Do you mean the shack is on this claim?"

"Yes," said the children together.

"Are you sure? How do you know?"

"Mr. Cleaver showed us where our stake is set; their shack is way this side."

Dick stuck his knife into a potato and stood up. "I'm going up to see about that."

"Oh, Dick, you're so tired. And the kids are probably mistaken about the shack. The boys were just teasing them."

"I'll feel better if I go up."

"Then I'm going with you. There are two of those boys, and I'm afraid you'll have trouble with them."

"You're going to do no such thing. It's no place for you."

"I'm afraid to have you go up there alone. There might be trouble."

"I don't expect any trouble, but I've got to see that shack."

"Then let me go, too."

Dick said no, with decision and emphasis, and Becky unwillingly had to agree. That new chivalry was a comfort and a joy, but it had its price. If Becky was to be given protection she must be willing to take it; she must not spoil this new feeling of responsibility by being too independent. "All right," she said meekly.

Dick's tall figure lumbered away through the twilight. Becky noticed, as she watched him go, that he had seemed to broaden out in the last few weeks. He was almost a man in size, and she was glad of it. He would need strength if at fifteen the protection of the family fell upon him.

The boy went through the tangled slough grass, crossed the creek, and climbed the hill to the spring. No one was in sight as he stooped to drink. The scolding water and a complaining wood dove made the only sounds he heard. Then over the hill a dog barked, and another dog answered. He climbed higher, following the sound, till he saw a light in a window. It came from a small shack standing on the hillside. It was a box of a house with one window and a stovepipe sticking through the roof; it was built of boards and covered with building paper that the wind had torn loose. The children were right. The shack certainly stood within the Linville boundary line.

As Dick approached two dogs began to strain at their leashes and bark madly. "Hello," he called, over the uproar.

The door opened, and a man and two half-grown boys appeared in the oblong of light.

"What you want?" demanded the man.

Dick ignored the surly tone. "I'm Linville," he said. "We're your new neighbors; just came yesterday. We found our pump out of order when we came, and we've been using the spring. When the children came up for water tonight they said some boys sent them off. I thought I'd come up and ask you if there was any reason why that spring shouldn't be used."

The boys snickered in a silly, awkward way. The father shook the ashes out of his pipe. "You're *right* there's a reason! I ain't furnishing water to trespassers."

"But I understood that the spring was on our land."

"Well, change your understanding, sonny; it 'taint. It's on mine."

"What section do you call yours?"

"Don't know any reason why you should be pinning me down to st'istics. But I'd as lieve tell you that this is Section twenty-three."

"But that's our claim."

The dogs moved up around his ankles. The man swore. "It is, is it? Well, I'll have you know, you young snapping turtle, that it's mine."

"But my uncle filed on twenty-three last fall, the night the land was thrown open."

"He's pretty late in getting his residence started. Why wasn't he around the first of March? That's when residence began."

"Because he was dying."

"He should 'a' come out here to die if he wanted the claim. He's lost it now; funerals don't cut no odds with the guv-ment. I been here since the first day of March, I got my crops in and witnesses to prove it, and plenty of neighbors to swear that there wasn't a rag of you folks around here on March first. Everybody thought you'd given up. I come in and plant my corn and make my

improvements, and then you show your sassy face
and claim the land's yours. You got a swell
chance of proving it! My advice to you is to
tell your folks to pull up stakes and git back
where they come from. If they stay around here
they're likely to git something more than a contest filed agin 'em."

The lighted doorway was full of heads. Back
of the man a woman's voice spoke a few words in
a low tone.

"You shut yer click," said her husband. "Keep
out o' what don't concern you." He turned to
Dick. "And as fer you, young feller, you get
out o' here, *quick*. Keep away from that spring
o' mine, and get off my land if you want to keep
out of trouble. I give you three days to pack
up; if you and your stealing family ain't out of
this section by that time there's going to be something doing around these parts!"

CHAPTER IV

TROUBLES

BECKY scarcely slept that night. The next morning, early, she and Dick were on their way to the Wubber claim, which lay to the north of what they had just begun to call home. The Wubbers' barn was built of sod, from which an occasional tuft of dried grass still waved in the breeze. The shack was of plank with a roof of corrugated iron which made a loud banging noise when the wind cut under its edges. There was a well and a chicken house and a "cave" in which the family kept their milk and butter, when Mrs. Wubber felt disposed to churn.

She was sitting in the open doorway in the only rocker — a large-framed woman, shaped very like her own churn. Gum in her mouth, an enormous man-sized pair of sandals on her stockingless feet, she was rocking and rocking and rocking. Her placidity and satisfaction with life was, somehow, an aggravation to the worried guests.

She did not rise from her chair to greet them, but her manner was cordial. "Come in, you-alls. You must be our new neighbors. Crystal, you and Autie bring two chairs. Set down and make yourselves easy-boned. Was you needin' your east cake?"

Dick told his errand, while Mrs. Wubber rocked and listened. The tow-headed children stood in groups around the three chairs. "Run and tell your paw who's here," she admonished them. "You got to take me just as I am," she told Becky, "I ain't got started at my work, yet." She caught Autumn around the neck, and gave him an indulgent spat. "Dirty boy, ain't had his face washed yet," she apologized fondly.

Mr. Wubber came in from the barn with a pail of milk in either hand. He set them in the corner, to the loud accompaniment of buzzing flies. Then he pulled up a soap box and sat down to listen to the story of the night before.

"That's Welp, all right," he said. "He's a mean cuss."

"Did you know he was living on our claim when you drove our goods out, yesterday?"

"Oh, yaas," said Mr. Wubber easily.

"Why didn't you tell us?"

"I hated to start you in with bad news. I ain't never seen his place, but I've seen him, and if he's as mean as he looks he's a terror. Trainer, his neighbor on the section south, has had a lot of trouble with him — lost chickens and tools and that kind of business."

"Has Welp been here long?"

"Well, he come out some time during the fall, I don't know just when. He put up such a poor kind of shack that nobody thought he was going to stick it out. When spring first came he brought his family up here from Gregory County, and did his planting, they tell me. Maybe now he intends to stay."

"Did he file at the land office?"

"I don't know anything about that. I heerd someone say, in the early winter, that he was going to contest your claim."

"Do you suppose he would have a chance of winning?"

"I don't know but he would, and I don't know *as* he would," said Mr. Wubber cheerily. "You never can tell what a president's going to decide. What are you — Republicans or Democrats?"

"Republicans."

"That's in your favor."

"I'd druther see *you* get it," remarked Mrs. Wubber. "Anyone can see that you-all have some refinement and been nice-raised. And that's the kind of neighbors I want for my childern — folks like ourselves."

"It's a good piece of land," said her husband. "It's worth fighting for. If I was you I'd scrap it out. Of course you wasn't on the land when you should 'a' been, this spring, but that wasn't your fault, and you probably got the death stifficate to prove it. Those Welps can make things pretty lively for you — they've got two cussed mean boys — but I'd stick it out if I was you."

"I wonder what the law would say about it."

"Dunno," said Mr. Wubber, "I ain't no lawyer; there ain't a law book in the house. Why don't you go to see someone that has one?"

"We haven't any money to spend on legal advice."

"Why don't you ask Cleaver about it? He's in the land business, as well as lumber, and has had a chance to hear of all kinds of contests. He's a white man, too; he'll advise you right."

Becky and Dick looked at each other. "We really haven't any time to spend on it," said the girl, more to her brother than to Mr. Wubber. "We ought to get in those potatoes, today. But we're so worried that we won't sleep till we know if our planting is all going to be wasted. I hate to lose two days, but I do think we'd better drive in to Dallas and see him, Dick."

"You won't have to go to Dallas if you go today," advised their neighbor.

"Why not?"

"Because he always spends this part of the week at Winner, ten miles north of here. He has his land office there."

"Let's go," said Dick.

Mrs. Wubber rocked comfortably back and forth, keeping time to the rocker with her gum. "Always best to start right at a job if it does put you out a bit," she approved.

"We'll have to go back and get the children," said Becky. "I'm afraid to leave them on the claim alone."

"Good luck to you," called Mr. Wubber, as they started back across the prairie. "If you get into a contest I'll be willing to testify that I seen your uncle pass my place the night he squatted."

THE Linville children found Mr. Cleaver in his office in the little flat town of Winner — a town set down like a toy village on the prairie. It was comforting to have an adult to consult, even though he gave them no definite encouragement.

"Too bad you're in for a contest," he said, when he heard their story. "I know this man Welp — he's a worthless sort of a villain — but I didn't know he'd squatted on your claim. If I had I'd have written your uncle advising you not to come out. You kids are too young to have a fight on your hands."

Becky looked worried, but Dick grinned. "We've had a lot of experience with scraps. There are four of us, you know."

"Not just this kind of scrap. Welp is a mean man to deal with."

"How much chance has he of winning?"

"That's hard to say. It's the Department of the Interior that will decide the case on its merits. Your uncle squatted in September, didn't he?"

"The last night of August."

"And he filed right away?"

"Yes, he crossed the line at midnight, drove his stakes, and set up his two-by-fours. Then he rode horseback to Gregory and filed his application at the land office."

"When did Welp come on the land?"

"We don't know. I can't believe he was here when Uncle Jim came back to build; he would certainly have seen him."

"How much improvement has he made?"

"Nothing built but a miserable little shack, and a rickety sort of a barn. But he has quite a lot of ground broken."

Mr. Cleaver drew circles on the blotter in front of him. "Of course you should have been on the land the first of March. The law says you must establish residence within six months of your filing."

"On the first of March Uncle wasn't able to speak a word."

"No doubt about your having a valid excuse for not coming. You certainly have justice on your side. But I've lived long enough to know that law is not always justice."

"What does the law say about contests?" asked Becky.

Mr. Cleaver wheeled in his chair and took down a red-bound book from the shelf.

"Are you a lawyer?" asked Phil.

"I'm a jack of all trades. I've been 'doctor, lawyer, merchant, chief,' since I landed in this neck of the woods. I've even done plumbing and plastering and read funeral services. You *have* to in new country. Here we are." He turned the pages to the place he wanted, and read aloud:

As between conflicting claims to public lands, he whose initiation is first in time, if adequately followed up, is deemed first in right.

"Well, that certainly was Uncle Jim," said Dick.

"Yes, the initiation; but how about the 'adequately followed up,'" asked Becky anxiously.

Mr. Cleaver went on:

. . . The first one acquiring actual, peaceable, physical possession of the location on unoccupied land of the United States, not reserved from such location, placing substantial improvements thereon, and continuing the same to completion . . . acquires the better right.

"I wouldn't call Welp's possession 'peaceable' so far," commented Dick. "I'll bet anything it was either he or his ole boys that broke our pump and windows."

. . . If, at any time after filing the affidavit . . . it is proved, after due notice to the settler,

to the satisfaction of the register of the land office, that the person having filed such affidavit has failed to establish residence within six months of the date of entry . . . the land so entered shall revert to the government.

"We never had any 'due notice,' " said Becky.

Mr. Cleaver turned back several pages:

Whenever a homestead entry has been made, followed by no settlement on the part of the one making that entry, and that homestead entry has, by lapse of time . . . been ended, anyone in actual possession as a settler and occupier of the land has a prior right to perfect title thereto.

"Gee," said Dick. "That looks bad for us, if I get the hang of those theretos."

Becky's face was tragic. "I hope Uncle Jim doesn't know about it."

Joan looked up from an enchanting paper weight which had held her speechless since her entrance to the office. It was a glass globe, in the heart of which were two tiny figures under an umbrella. When you shook the weight a blizzard of snowflakes fell fast and furious on the little couple, who withstood the elements with happy smiles. She laid the fascinating thing back on Mr. Cleaver's desk. "Are the Welpses going to take the creek away from us?" she asked.

"Not if we have anything to say about it," said Mr. Cleaver heartily. "You'll learn to swim in that creek yet, Joan." Then he turned to the two older children. "Don't begin to worry about things. I don't have much idea that man can ever take that claim away from you. What the government wants is the assurance that the settler intends to make of the land a real homestead, and you would have no trouble proving that your uncle took up the claim with that idea. In the second place, I doubt that Welp could ever raise money enough to pay for a contest. That's expensive business, and he's a worthless no-account loafer, who has no credit left anywhere in this part of the country. How he got his breaking done I don't see. I don't think he'd ever have the energy to plow it himself. How much breaking have *you* got?"

"Only about fifteen acres, which were plowed

last fall. Uncle Jim didn't want us to try farming. He said that if we ran the garden and got enough corn for the animals we'd be doing well. And even if we did want to break more, we couldn't; we have no plow and we can't afford to hire it done. We'll do well to take care of what we have."

"Well," advised Mr. Cleaver, "if you can't prove 'substantial improvements' by cultivated land, you'll have to do it in some other way. I judge from your description of the Welp shack that it's no palace — "

"We'd call it a chicken house, back in Platteville," said Phil.

"And their barn is probably nothing but a shanty. Unless they put in more money than I think they possess they'll find it hard to convince Uncle Sam that it is a permanent home. I have an idea that they'll melt away in the fall before cold weather sets in, but of course we can't count on that. What you kids must do is to set to work to make that place of yours look like a home. Get things growing around it, and a few trees started. Maybe later in the year you can fence

a small part of it.   Keep your ground as neat as
you can — the prairie wind will help you with
that.   Then if your neighbor files his contest
we'll send kodak pictures of the two places to
Washington, and we'll *see* Welp get it!"

"But we haven't time to do all that, now," said
Dick.   "We're way behind with our garden,
and we have to get that planted or we'll have
nothing to eat next year.   We're not settled in
the house — just barely moved in; all that corn
has to be planted; and the potatoes — why Mr.
Cleaver, you haven't any idea how many potatoes we four eat!"

Becky opened her eyes wider.   Astonishment
was written all over her face.   Was this Dick
Linville, the track team captain, talking about
keeping the larder full next winter?

"Well, you don't have to do everything in a
minute," comforted Mr. Linville.   "Get your
garden planted first, just as your uncle planned;
then go at your corn.   The other improvements
can wait; you'll probably be at them all summer.
As for your being behind time, you may be late
according to the calendar, but not much accord-

ing to the weather. Dakota is not Wisconsin, you know. On the first of May we had a two days' blizzard here last year."

Becky looked comforted. "If we can do it a little at a time it won't be so hard."

"Well, that's the way to go at it — day by day. If you start too strong in the beginning you'll be sick, and that won't help you along. Let the settling of your house go for a few weeks till your planting's done. In the meantime can't you get a tree or two started around the house? Go down to that little thicket that is on the edge of your land and see if you can't find an aspen or a cotton-wood that is small enough to transplant. They grow rapidly, and nothing makes a place look civilized as fast as a tree."

"I'll get a half dozen," promised Dick.

"Hold on, young man; wait until you've tried to dig a hole for them in that wild-rose-y soil. You'll think one is enough then. Get everything around the place looking as habitable as you can, and some day, when your vines and your fig trees are started, I'll come out and take a picture of the claim. Then if that Welp — he certainly is named right! — files a contest on us, we'll be ready for him."

The word "us" went straight to Becky's heart. Dakota seemed less large and lonesome and the Linvilles less stranded if there was someone with them. "I don't know how we can ever thank you for this advice."

"Nonsense," laughed Mr. Cleaver. "Who doesn't *love* to give advice? Besides, you'll probably never need it; I haven't much fear of Welp filing a contest. My only worry is that he and his worthless family will make trouble for you all summer. Of course they can if they're so disposed. However, we needn't borrow any trouble. Go your own way, pay no attention to his threats, and if his kids come around your place untie the dog."

"I wish we had one," said Becky.

"No dog?"

"No, Uncle Jim told us to get one as soon as we could. We'd love a dog."

"Well, stop worrying about things. I don't believe we're going to lose that claim, but of course we don't want to be caught napping. If you want to keep it — you're sure you *do* want to, aren't you?"

"*Sure!*" chorused the four voices.

"Then you all set to work to make it look just as much like home as you can. You've had a home, and you ought to know how they look, better than the Welp family, who have never had a real one. Sister, do you like that glass blizzard?"

Joan smiled one of her rare smiles.

"Then you put it in your pocket and take it along home with you. You probably aren't used to prairie wind, so you don't know that no Dakota claim is complete without a paper weight."

The children rose to go. "Hold on," said Mr. Cleaver, "If you'll wait for a moment I'll drive out to the edge of town with you; I have an errand out that way."

"We have a few errands here ourselves," said Becky. "Table oilcloth, and safety pins and sticky fly paper; all things that are zero in shopping trips. But there are a trillion flies in the shack, and they drive us crazy."

"All right," said Mr. Cleaver. "Say we meet

in front of my office in half an hour; that'll give us both time."

They found him waiting in the wagon when they returned with their bundles. He laid on Becky's lap a number of bright-colored envelopes. "For your garden, Mistress Mary. Coreopsis and cornflowers to sow broadcast, and some cosmos to try. The coreopsis grows wild out here: it ought to do well."

Joan gave his arm a shy squeeze. "You seem like Platteville," she said. And Mr. Cleaver looked as though he understood.

On the outskirts of the town he went into a farm yard, leaving the children outside. When he came back a dog followed him, a large, reddish dog, with an intelligent head and bright eyes. He whistled to it, and patted the wagon box invitingly. The animal leaped in, wagging his tail at the exclamation of the children.

"There's your dog," said Mr. Cleaver. "Two years old; part collie and part shepherd. Well trained for cows, and safe with kids. I only hope he won't be safe for everybody else. Now I'll feel easier about you. Speak up, Bronx, and

salute your new family; you're going home."
And with a wave of his hand, Mr. Cleaver turned
back to Winner. He stopped before he reached
the turn in the road. "Hey," he called. Dick
drew up the horses.

"If you have any more trouble let me know."

THE wagon bumped along over the trail which
ran like a parting between two hairy stretches of
buffalo grass. Wild roses made a mat of color
along the roadway; not a faint pink, like Platteville roses, but a vivid rose-color that was almost
red. Here and there a slope of snow-on-the
mountain made white waves in the sea of green,
and meadow phlox were blots of violet ink in the
grass. Now and then they drove by homely little
houses of sod or unpainted boards, bare and lonesome looking, with nothing to shade them or
soften their rude outlines. Most of them had a
door and a window; some of them had pumps;
each one had a section of rusty stovepipe sticking out of the roof. Wherever there were children a flock of sunburned boys and girls, with

bare brown legs and faded hair, ran out to see the Linvilles pass.

One boy had a dead snake, with dust-colored checks on its back, tied to a pole. The snake looked like a huge whip-lash, as he threw it after the wagon. Near one shack was chained a coyote, with a snarling mouth and shifting eyes, and the children had to hold Bronx to keep him from leaping out for a visit. Around each small shack there was a clearing, and in each one of these fields that looked like black patches on the green, a homesteader was plowing or planting. If his ground ran up hill, his black figure looked like a shadow picture against the blue sky.

Joan regretted the stretches of breaking. They were like torn patches on skin, she said, and she was sure the prairie didn't like being cut up, that way. "It proba'ly hates people coming out here to stick shovels into it," she remarked, jolting about in the wagon.

"I guess it'd rather have shovels stuck into it than tomahawks," argued Phil.

"About the same thing," retorted his sister. "That's what plowing is — scalping the prairie."

Phil took a virtuous turn: "It proba'ly prefers being useful and raising corn to running wild with roses."

"*Yes,* it does! Raising corn is like going to school; raising wild roses is playing Saturdays. Don't tell *me* which one it perfers!"

"Quit your arguing," said Dick from the front seat. "Don't you kids *ever* get tired of scrapping?"

Phil knew the perfect retaliation. "Bronx is going to be mine," he said, pulling the dog on to his lap.

"He's all of ours," retorted Joan. "Mr. Cleaver said so." She turned the glass globe lovingly in her hands, making the snowflakes fly. "He's not like the paper weight, which belongs just to me."

It was long past noon when the wagon drove up in front of the house. Becky went in to get lunch while Dick unharnessed the team. She heard him call from the barn and hurried out to hear.

"Red Haw has got away," he said. Red Haw was the cow that the children had christened the first day on the claim.

"Where did you leave her?"

"Staked out back of the barn."

"Could she have pulled away? That stake was a long one."

"I don't see how; I drove it way into the ground. But stake and all are gone. Do you suppose she's gone back home?"

"Goodness, I hope not," said Becky, looking worried. "Maybe she followed down the creek looking for better grass. We'll go out hunting after lunch."

"Perhaps I ought to start now."

But Becky insisted that they eat first. No telling how long they might have to hunt after the lost cow. After lunch Dick put a saddle on the horse and followed the course of the creek westward. Becky took the two children and climbed the hill back of the house. From there she could see for miles across the green grass. No cow was in sight. She had half suspected their troublesome neighbors, but she could see every inch of the Welp barnyard, and no animal was there.

Dick returned in an hour without the cow. No one that he had questioned had seen her.

"Did you go up by the Welps?" asked Becky.

"No, but I was telling Mr. Trainer about Red Haw's being missing when the Welp boy rode past his gateway. Trainer called to him to know if he'd seen anything of a red cow. The Welp boy pointed at me. '*His* cow?' he said. Trainer said 'yes.' 'The cow knows enough not to stay on a claim that doesn't belong to her,' he said, and rode away, laughing. Guess I'd better try the east hills," and he started in the other direction with a sinking heart. Without the cow the food question became a serious one.

Meanwhile Becky and the two children scoured the claim. Becky felt sure that they would find her in the deep slough grass that lay along the creek, but no Red Haw was there, though they followed the banks for a couple of miles.

"I'll bet the Welps have her," said Phil. Becky echoed the thought, but she didn't dare admit it, even to herself.

"Perhaps she wandered back to her old home."

"But the people who sold her said that she always came in to be milked."

Becky did not answer. She tried to think of what hopeful things Uncle Jim would have said, but her heart felt like a weight in her chest. How would they ever get through the year without milk? And they could not afford to buy another Red Haw.

The shadows had begun to lengthen when Dick returned. He came back empty-handed and discouraged. He had ridden miles along the creek-bed, hunting and inquiring, without a crumb of comfort.

"I'm going to turn in early," he said, as he washed his dusty face and hands before his supper was eaten. "I s'pose I've got to ride into Dallas tomorrow and see if that fool cow has wandered back home. That'll be another day wasted."

"We'll work while you're gone," comforted Becky. "The children and I can finish the potatoes."

Dick laid an old piece of sacking in the box that the children had hunted out for a home for Bronx, and called the dog.

"Oh, can't he stay in the house," begged Phil. "I'm afraid he'll run off, too."

"If he runs off he'll have to run. I don't expect to spend my life teaching animals where their own fireside is," said Dick gruffly. "Besides, I want him out-of-doors to greet any sneak thieves that happen by."

Sometime in the night Becky was awakened by a bark, followed by the sound of heavy feet swishing through the grass. She got out of bed and went to the window. A cover of blue-black sky, alight with stars, cupped the earth. The wind had gone down and the prairie was so still that she could almost hear the silence. The last quarter of a moon shone full on the slope above her, and down the white trail trotted two figures. Red Haw was ahead, and at her heels, dusty and dew-drenched, with drooping tail, came Bronx.

The girl roused Dick, who put on enough clothes to go out and receive the lost member of the family. Becky slipped on shoes and shawl, and followed him out to the barn. Red Haw was already crouched on the straw, evidently weary from her trip.

"No wandering off about that," said Dick indignantly. "She's been milked, and the stake and rope are gone. And it was our brand new rope. Somebody's had a hand in that."

"Never mind the rope as long as the cow is back. Where do you suppose they hid her?"

"Bronx knows. Probably somewhere in the deep grass, for they're both drenched with dew."

"But how did he find her? He never knew there *was* a cow here."

"Ask me something easier. Maybe he smelled her about the place and knew she wasn't in the barn where cows belong. Maybe he just stumbled upon her by accident. Anyway, she's here."

"I'm going to feel a lot safer with him around."

"So am I." Dick stooped down and patted the dog. Then he locked the barn door, and the three walked back to the house together. Bronx crept in on the sacking and turned himself around twice before he settled down for the night.

Becky patted his wet fur. "It isn't going to be so easy to steal cows after this," she said.

The frogs were still croaking when she dropped back to sleep.

CHAPTER V

MAKING A HOME

A T THE close of almost every page in Uncle
Jim's book he had added the words: *Stop
work just before you get tired*. Becky's eyes
never failed to soften when she read them, but she
sometimes smiled too. For it couldn't be done.
How *could* one apportion work that came crowd-
ing in so fast that you had no time to plan? The
tasks marched in a long, unending procession, so
many and so heavy that the housework slipped
into second place, and often had to be left to the

younger children. Becky and Dick were up almost as early as the sun. They dug and hoed and planted. They put in potatoes and melons; they planted a little alfalfa; on the overturned sod they dropped their field corn. They did it with the confidence born of youth; if they had been a few years older they would have been more timorous and less hopeful. They built a chicken house, and a shelter for the dog. They set out currant bushes, and raspberries and rhubarb; they laid boards from their packing boxes for a rude sidewalk in the back door yard. And whenever there was a momentary lull in the outside work there was always bread to be mixed, beans to be baked, or clothes to be washed.

The out-of-door living and the hard physical work gave them appetites that could hardly be satisfied, and it seemed to Becky that she never got her family quite filled up. Once a week Dick went to town for supplies, which seemed enormous but which she could scarcely stretch to last the seven days. Careful as she tried to be, the money seemed to flow away, and the two older children could hardly wait for the garden to relieve their purse. But there was no time for worry, even; during the day there was too much work, and when night came they fell asleep the moment they touched their pillows.

There were no more meetings with the Welp family. After Red Haw's return they saw no more of outlawry. The children had been warned to keep away from the troublesome neighbors and to avoid the spring, and the presence of the dog made Becky feel that their own home was guarded. Bronx was a fine policeman. At the slightest word of affection from his own family he would quiver all over with delight; his tail would wag nervously as he awaited their praise or blame, and his liquid eyes would seek theirs, pathetically eager for an invitation. But at the approach of a stranger his hair would stiffen along his back, and a growl would start that seemed to come from the very depth of his stomach. His bark heralded the coming of a visitor long before the family could either hear or see the arrival, and with him on the front doorstep Becky felt relieved and safe.

The dewiness and freshness of spring time had

turned into flaming summer, and the sun baked in at the kitchen window as Becky mixed her breakfast pancakes. She called to her brother as she stirred the batter:

"You'll have to get some more flour today, Dick. I'll have to scrape the bottom of the can to set sponge tonight."

Dick was bringing in the big bucket of warm milk which did so much to supply their table. "Flour? I thought we started with two hundred and fifty pounds."

"We did. But one sack is gone, and the field mice got into the others."

Dick sighed. "It's the unexpected things like mice and hail and measles that cost. But of course we've got to have flour; I'll go into town this morning."

There was an excited duet from Joan and Phil, "Oh, may we go too?"

"I guess so. You've been pretty fair kids about sticking to the garden, and you've earned a day off. But I won't have any fighting."

"Then you'd better leave Joan home," suggested Phil.

"Or take out Phil's bronnical tubes," retorted Joan.

"What for, I'd like to know?"

"So he couldn't talk; bronnical tubes are what you speak through."

"Hoh, hoh!" jeered Phil. *"Speaking* through bronnical tubes! Those tubes are what you get sore throat in. I just knew how it would be if you were let to go; we'd be sure to have a quarrel."

Becky called the children into separate rooms to be cleaned, while she helped with their clothes and put up their lunch. "Seems nice to see you in something besides overalls," she said, as she helped Phil into a clean blouse. "Dick, you'll have to get this boy a new pair of shoes today. His toes are out."

"What do you do, *eat* your shoes?" demanded Dick. "I never saw anyone go through cowhide the way you and Joan do. You'll have to go barefoot the rest of the summer."

"Suits *me* all right."

"It doesn't suit me," said Becky. "If you don't wear shoes you'll look just like every other squatter's child."

"Why *not* look that way? That's what I am."

Well, *why* not, Becky wondered. It would save the expense of shoes. They were claim-dwellers now; they must live like squatters. You could not carry the standards of Platteville on to the prairies. The bare feet were a symbol; they seemed like a letting down, a sag in living. And yet it was the practical, the best thing to do. "Guess you're right, Dick," she said. "I wouldn't get the shoes."

As soon as the family departed Becky hurried through her housework. She had a plan for that day. No dinner to get; no gardening; no building; at least six hours without interruption, and she knew what she wanted to do with that time. She called Bronx, took a wooden box with a rope tied to it, and went up the stony hill behind the house.

It was a bleak, bare hillside where nothing grew but the mulleins and the buffalo grass that poked coarse tufts up between the flat rocks that covered the sides. At the summit it was almost all stone. The wind up there was so strong that it blew Becky's skirts straight out behind her, and when she called to Bronx she could not hear her own voice. She stopped a moment to look across the prairie, which seemed each day to hold a new appeal. The deep grass below her had russet spots on it, now and then, a soft, reddish glow, like the bloom of a peach. The rim of the sky cut down over the earth like a cookie cutter. "Boom, boom," called a prairie cock from the deep grass, and a hawk swept lazily through the blueness above her. She looked at the billowing miles below her with a softened expression on her face before she turned to work among the rocks at her feet.

From the stones she selected large, flat shapes until she filled her box. She drew them down hill, steadying the box with her hand, and dumped them in a pile at the front door. Three times she returned for more. Then from the door to the edge of the natural terrace on which the house stood, she strung a taut line, and followed it with a spade, leaving behind her an irregular row of shallow holes into which she laid the flat rocks. These made stepping stones to the trail, and to the spot where they would some day have a fence, and perhaps even a gate.

Along the stepping stones, at either side, she dug long, narrow beds for flowers, ending at Castor and Pollux. It was the hardest work Becky had ever undertaken, for it was in virgin soil, untouched by plow or harrow. It meant digging through the tough prairie sod, through the net-work of roots that lay below, till the black loam was exposed. Each clump of root had to be lifted and shaken to remove the earth that clung to it, then thrown down to the creek bed below. Some day those clods would help to build a dam. The prairie sun baked down fiercely; when she looked up from the ground its white light was almost blinding. Perspiration streamed down her face, her hands were stiffened by soil and roughened by rocks, but she stuck stoutly to the task which was to accomplish so much in home-making.

At noon when she stopped for lunch she was so hot that the thought of food was not tempting. The inevitable fried bacon, potatoes, and canned vegetables offered little inducement to eat. She longed for a melon, or oranges, or a salad that should be crisp and cool. "How I used to hate the sound of those ice wagons rumbling by in Platteville," she said to herself, "and how far I'd run to hear one now!" She got butter from the well, spread several slices of thin bread, and opened a can of tomatoes. That was the best Tripp County could offer in coolness and freshness.

Down the long beds she went with her seeds in the early afternoon. She hoed and raked the ground until it fell apart into fine grains of loam; then she threw the seed broadcast — coreopsis and cornflowers and cosmos and poppies. At the end of the walk she planted a row of sunflowers at right angles to her garden. They might cast a little shade in the hot days that were to come, and their seeds would save chicken feed.

On the side of the house that faced the creek she dug two deep holes. It took her nearly an hour to get through the grass, the tough soil, and the roots below. Then she walked a half mile to one of the tiny thickets that bordered the creek. It was no grove — just a handful of small dwarf ashes, box elders, and cottonwoods that had sprung up on its banks. "At home they'd call these 'brush,' and thin them all out," thought Becky, sitting down for a moment to rest luxuriously in real shade. "But how wonderful they are here! And where did the seed that started them come from? We're miles from a tree of any size."

She longed to transplant one of the taller ones, but common sense told her that she would be more successful with a sapling. So she picked out a tiny aspen and a baby ash, carried water from the creek to pour about their roots, and dug deep around them. She took them up with a large clump of earth at each base, wrapped the roots in old sacking, and carried them one at a time, to her wheelbarrow. And then hot, tired, but triumphant, she wheeled her prizes through the burning sun to their new home. So large was the mass of soil that clung to them that she was able to get them into the ground without disturbing their roots. The leaves had not withered, the tiny branches stuck out boldly, and when the last spadeful of earth went in around them they seemed to have grown in their new surroundings. The aspen leaves quivered in the wind, and there on the prairie was a real spot of shade. Becky laid an earth-stained hand on the trunk. "Grow fast," she said.

It was hot in the house too, but the relief from the sun was a comfort. Becky pulled out the smoothest of the packing boxes into which Uncle Jim had put shelves and rubbed in the green stain that was left from the floor borders. The shelves in the room and the two wicker chairs got a coat of the same color. The white curtains which she had never had time to hang were brought out and strung on wires above the windows. She covered the living-room cot with the green cretonne, flowered in orange and blue, that she had bought in Dallas; slipped the pillow into an orange casing, and added another pillow covered with dull blue. She unpacked the books and stood them in the stained packing case, rejoicing over them as old friends. She took the victrola out of its straw packings and moved it into the living-room, putting Dick's ukulele on the table shelf below. Over the kitchen table oilcloth she laid a square of spotless linen. "More to wash, but I'm not going to have us living like heathen," she said to herself, almost fiercely. She brought a jar of wild sunflowers for the table and another for the bookcase. Then she stood off and surveyed the result of her work. "Perhaps Uncle Jim wouldn't like the couch coverings," she said. "He might call them 'gimcracks.' But bare boards have to be dolled up some way. Anyway, it looks cosy."

She gave herself the luxury of a leisurely bath, soaking her abused hands in hot water till they were almost smooth. Then she exchanged one of the dark blue calicoes that she had worn ever since she had reached the claim, for a clean green-and-white gingham. And then, oh joy, she sat down in the deep red chair that had come by freight a few days before, and took out the first book she had touched since she had stepped into Tripp County. At least an hour to read and rest and invite one's soul, with nothing driving her, indoors or out. She opened her "Oxford Book of Verse" with delight as well as hunger. How she would read!

Her lame shoulders settled back into the comfortable depths of the chair. The flies droned outside the screen door. The wind blew through the rooms — a wind that stirred, but did not cool, the air . . . The book closed in her hands; her head drooped. She was back in Platteville with Aunt Jule telling her that she was too big a girl to walk on stilts . . .

Bronx gave a warning bark and started up the trail, woofing loudly as he went. Becky started, and picked up the book which had fallen to the floor. It was prairie again, not Platteville. She ran to the door, half expecting to see a Welp come down the road.

A lean, sorrel horse ambled over the hill with two people on his back. He came down the Linville trail, and his driver reined him in at the side of the house. She was a gaunt, weatherbeaten woman with thin wisps of faded hair flying about her face. Her shoulder blades thrust out the back of her dress; great cords stuck out when she moved her neck. A little girl sat in front of her. "You seen anything of a white horse?" called the woman.

Becky hurried out to the trail.   It seemed good to have a visitor, even one who came hunting a horse.

"He's been missing since yestiddy noon," said the woman.   "Last time we seen him he was out eatin', and when we looked again he was gone. We started out after him early this morning, but we ain't seen hide er hair of him."

"We lost our cow the same way a few weeks ago," said Becky.

"Where'd you find her?"

Becky explained the cow's mysterious return.

"Was she an all-red cow with a white nose?"

"Yes."   Becky described Red Haw and her rope.

"I bet I seen that cow.   The Welp boy was milkin' her along the creek-bed one afternoon. I don't hold no truck with those Welpses so I didn't speak to him, but I know right well they ain't got no cow now."

"Why didn't they keep her after they got hold of her?"

"Oh, they wouldn't dast do that.   Folks has been lynched for less'n stealing a cow.   They probably pulled up her stake so's to make trouble for you an' then stole your rope. They're a thieving, low-down set, those Welpses. I never seen a meaner boy than that Pete."

"Do you suppose they have your horse?"

"No, I went along that way to look, first thing. No horse there, and no place to hide one, less'n they put him behind their tin can pile. That's most big enough to shelter an animal. No, they're mean enough to steal anything, but I reckon they didn't do it, this time."

"Won't you come in and rest a few minutes?"

The woman hesitated. "Oh, do. Let's, ma," begged the little girl.

"I don't know but we might as well. There ain't much of any place left to hunt; I been all around the creek. I guess the Mister'll have to start out tomorrow when he gets back from town." She got out of the man's saddle, and lifted the little girl down. "She's plum tuckered out, riding in this hot sun."

The child raised a pair of violet eyes, fringed by dark lashes, to Becky's face. They were her one beauty; her pinched little face was the face of a cripple, and her back bent in an unmistakable spinal curvature.

Rejoicing in her day of work, Becky led the way into the house. The woman gave a sweeping glance of appraisal about the room; the little girl showed open delight in her surroundings. "You sure got it nice here," she said.

"My name is Rebecca Linville. What's yours?" asked the hostess.

"Marietta Kenniker."

"We're new homesteaders, so we don't know the neighborhood yet. Do you live near us?"

"We live in the sod house two miles up the creek, past the Welpses. We seen your things when you drove past our place. You had bed springs."

"Marietta never seen bed springs before except when she was to the hospital," explained her mother.

"Do you like homesteading?"

Marietta shook her head. "It's too lonesome."

"Haven't you any brothers or sisters to play with?"

"Marietta's all," said the woman. "I had nine, but she's the only one left. And she the way she is!"

A slow flush crept over the little girl's face. Becky melted with pity. She brought out bread and strawberry jam, made from the Platteville garden. She gave the child Joan's doll to hold. "This belongs to my little sister," she said. "She's about as old as you."

"How old is she?"

"Eight."

"I'm twelve. I've stopped playing with dolls. But I look like eight."

"She wasn't born that way," explained Mrs. Kenniker. "She had a fall when she was a baby. She's always been pindly. But I don't know but it's a good thing; if she'd been well she'd be worked to death. That's what always happens to women folks on the prairies."

"Have you lived here long?"

"I've lived in Dakoty fifteen years. Come here when I was first married, from Kansas. I was sixteen then. I've homesteaded twict — once before, in Gregory County."

"Why did you leave your claim there to come to new land?"

"Oh, it wasn't ours. We proved up on it, but we couldn't pay for it; the bank got it."

Becky tried not to show her astonishment. Fifteen years. That made her thirty-one years old. Could this gaunt woman, with the hollow eyes and the yellow skin drawn tightly across her cheeks, be only thirty-one? She looked sixty.

"So you thought you'd try it again."

"The Mister did. I didn't want to come. I'm like Marietta here; I hate the prairie."

The little girl turned her sober eyes upon her mother. She had laid down the doll and was looking at the rows of books in the new bookcase.

"It's beautiful country," commented Becky.

"Oh yes, it's likely country all right — in the springtime. But that fresh grass is just like a false face. You wait till the green goes and the blizzards come, and *then* see what you think about it! It's bare everywhere, and the sky shuts you down just like a cover. There's no gettin' away from it. And the wind blows all the time; it nags at you till it finally gets you. I ain't got no love for the prairies."

"Then why did you come?"

"Oh, the Mister he's cracked about it. The prairie seems to make him drunk, you might say. The minute he seen this land opening advertised he was crazy to come. I know just how it's going to end: we're going to put in five years of nigger's work, and starvin', and lonesomeness, and no schoolin' for Marietta, and then the bank'll get it all. But you can't make *him* believe that. When you've got the prairie in your blood you can't get it out."

Becky's quick brain revolved the woman's words. That was the way this new country had attracted Uncle Jim; that was the way it had affected her. There *was* a call of the prairie, sure enough. It had drawn her, just as it had drawn Uncle Jim, and the Mister. She wondered if the prairie woman was right — if these green promises would never be realized; if the springtime face that the prairie showed — the life, the sparkle, the color — was only a mask to lure the unwary.

"I suppose it *is* lonely in the winter."

"It's just like lookin' at an empty cupboard," said Mrs. Kenniker. "There ain't nothin' there. You look out your window as soon as snow flies, and you see just miles of nothin'. And that prairie wind keeps agoin' and agoin' all the time. You know it's the wind and nothin' but the wind, and you say to yourself that you ain't agoin' to give in to it. But it keeps at you till it finally gits you."

Becky looked her sympathy.

"I ain't acarin' about me," went on Mrs. Kenniker. "I'm usen to it, now. But Marietta's stuck out here where she ain't gittin' no schoolin'. She ought to be fillin' her head up, because she ain't never goin' to be able to use her arms 'n her legs. And she's awful smart about books; she reads everything she lays hands on."

The child had drawn her chair close to the bookcase, and was looking at the shelves with hungry eyes. "You got a lot of books." She looked at her mother eagerly. "I'm going to ask *her* if she knows." She indicated Becky.

"Yes, do," urged Mrs. Kenniker.

"Have you got a book called 'Little Women'?"

"Oh, dear," said Becky. "I did have it, but it isn't out here with us. It was worn to rags, and we left it in Platteville when we came away."

Marietta looked her disappointment. "Did you read it?"

"Oh, many times. I loved it when I was your age."

"I started it once," said Marietta. "The doctor's little girl had it when I was at the hospital in Sioux City, and she let me take it. I read up to the place where Beth falls in the skating pond. Then I got too sick to read, and when I was able to sit up again she had gone away, and taken the book with her. That was two years ago, and I never knew how it turned out. I've ast and ast everybody I've seen. Can't *you* tell me what came after that? I was just crazy about that book!"

And Becky told her, struggling to remember the details, of Amy's painting experiences, of Jo's attempts at writing, of Beth's final illness, of the coming together of Laurie and Amy, of Jo's romance. And as she saw the hunger in the child's eyes, and the eagerness with which she followed the story, she realized what prairie living meant to the people that could never get away from it. It was a prison. There seemed no verge to its boundless sweeps, the sky that bent over it was its only limit, but it was a prison just the same. Her heart overflowed with pity for the mother and the little girl, and she pressed "Polly Oliver's Problem" and "Greek Heroes" into Marietta's hands at parting, with an offer to lend her more books later.

Mrs. Kenniker looked her gratitude. "We got something good on this trip, if it *wasn't* a horse," she said, as she took up her reins and started off.

BECKY got the food ready for the Linville supper, then sat down on the back step of the house to await her family. The wind had dropped, as it always did about sundown, the air was cooler, and the prairie looked subdued and peaceful. A striped gopher ran out of his hole and approached almost to the girl's feet. A mourning dove called out its plaintive, haunting note.

The sunshine lay like a warm smile on the ground, and the air was still and sweet. It was hard to believe, in the face of that quiet and serenity, that the prairie could ever betray her.

She heard the wagon coming while it was still far off, and saw Bronx's tawny figure dashing down the trail to meet it. The children were singing, and Job and Methus were trotting along at a lively pace. It was too bad that the family were returning from that direction, so that her improvements could not burst upon them unannounced, but she would not let them miss anything. "Drive around the house," she called as they approached.

"What for?"

"You'll see."

The wagon jolted around the house, the three passengers looking eagerly over the side. One by one they took in the changes, the new flower beds, the new walk, and — wonder of all — the new trees.

"You *have* made a day of it!" said Dick.

"Glad I wasn't here to be made to carry those stones!" commented Phil.

But Joan went to the little aspen tree, looked up into its shaking, shining leaves and said nothing.

They were delighted with the living-room, and did not hesitate to say so. The victrola and the books were welcomed with shrieks of joy, and even the green gingham dress came in for its share of approval. Becky felt conscience-stricken as she saw their pleasure. "I've been so busy homesteading that I've let the home-making go," she thought to herself. "I must change that; I've got to keep up both ends."

"Needn't think you're the only one that's been planning improvements," said Dick, coming from the barn with his arms full. "Just cast your eye over this." He laid down on the door step a pile of green-and-white striped canvas, with an occasional rod of metal sticking through.

"It looks like an awning," said Becky.

"Good guess," replied her brother. "That's just what it is. Mr. Cleaver has had a new window cut in his land office at Winner, and the window's too big for the old awning. I offered to buy it to keep that south sun out of our window, but he wouldn't take anything for it. He said the awning would take the wear and tear off the castor beans; they wouldn't have to grow so fast to shade you, and that it was no good to him. He put it into my wagon box before I could refuse it. I'll get it up tomorrow."

"Bet it's the only awning on the Rosebud Reservation," exulted Phil.

"Seems like Platteville here tonight," said Joan. "I wish Uncle Jim could see it."

CHAPTER VI

THE ENEMY ATTACKS

WHEN BECKY had been packing the toys Uncle Jim had advised her not to take too many. "All the books the children own," he had said. "Joan's doll, a baseball and bat, and some board games for the long, winter evenings."

"But what will they do in the summer time?" she had asked.

"Don't worry about that; the prairie itself is a pastime. If I know my kids — and I think I do — they'll never be bored a minute. When they

get time to play they'll do it without toys. The
land itself is a background for any pretend in the
world."

And Becky learned that he was right. The
hard work in which the children had to share
made playtime more attractive than it had ever
before been to them, and when the weeding, the
chores and the dishes were done they never asked:
"What shall we do?"

For there were so many things calling to be
done. The creek-bed was a place of eternal fascination. Where it ran swift and deep between
narrow banks there were snail shells and queer
water-hyacinths and bright-colored pebbles.
Where it widened into broad pools there were
blunt-nosed suckers and frogs and turtles. A
black-and-white-nosed badger lived in a hole
near the creek's edge, and tortoises as big as the
bottom of a dish pan lumbered along its banks.
On the big stone hill snakes lay about and sunned
themselves on the flat rocks. The fact that the
children were forbidden to go there alone only
added extra fascination to the place. They dared
not disobey, but they never passed by without

throwing a stone up the hill in the hope of dislodging a yellow-and-brown bull snake or a diamond-backed rattler from his sun porch.

There was always the prairie dog town to visit, where Bronx lived in perpetual hope of catching one of the scolding little beasts. They invariably waited, while he ran barking madly up to them; then at the last moment disappeared suddenly into their homes, with a last defiant yap. There was not the slightest chance of his getting one, but he never gave up the hope, and each time started after them with his original spirit and zest. The excitement of the chase was always at hand, for when there were not prairie dogs there were chipmunks, everywhere, cotton-tails showing their white backs ahead of you, and an occasional jack rabbit that always took to the hills when pursued. His hind legs were so long that a dog had no chance with him in a race, for he ran faster on a slope than on the level. "There goes an ole jack, back-legging himself up the hill," Joan used to say.

The long slough grass was a delightful place to wander, for after the meadow lilies and the buffalo peas were gone, wild larkspur and golden coreopsis made splashes of color on its surface. As you walked through it, giant grasshoppers jumped ahead of you in clouds, and now and then a meadow-lark, who waited until you were almost upon her, darted up from her nest on the ground.

Down on the edge of the creek the children had built a small "homestead" of their own, and it was here that they played oftenest during the hot summer days. Together they had cleared a space on which they placed the tiny farm buildings that they had made out of old boxes. It was a complete claim outfit: with house, barn, shed, several wagons, a hay-cart and, most wonderful of all, a windmill that went round and round in the breeze that never failed. Their little farm was the delight of their hearts, and there was no limit to the games that could be played, with it as a background. The doll and the baseball were untouched, and Becky, while she bemoaned the clay on the overalls, rejoiced at the sunburn on the faces and the flesh that grew on the thin legs.

The young Linvilles had helped Becky "get the wash out" in the early morning, and had just started to play in their little settlement when the Wubber children arrived.

The three oldest had walked over the burning prairie trail, wheeling the baby, Twinkle, in a home-made wagon.

"Pa and Ma is hoin' the corn," announced Autumn, joyfully. "She said we could stay till we fit."

They lifted Twinkle out of the conveyance, and set her upon the ground. A single garment of blue calico hung about the baby limply.

"Ain't you afraid of ants on her?" inquired Joan maternally.

"She's used to bites," said Crystal. "They's flies on her all the time."

The baby sat stolidly staring at them with her round blue eyes. There were tangles in her duck-tails of sunburned hair and traces of molasses about her mouth, but to Joan, hungry for the Platteville babies to mother, she was a welcome visitor. She cuddled her up beside her while they all played "claim." Presently Autumn offered to show Phil a place where ground cherries grew, and the two wandered off over the prairie together. Then "claim" became "house," and Joan assumed maternal charge of a family of three.

"I'll tell you what, le's wash the baby," she suggested.

"What for? We ain't goin' no wheres."

"'Cause she's so dirty; she'd be real nice-looking if she had that crust off of her."

"I'm afraid she'd take cold."

"Oh, no she won't. It's too hot to take cold. We'll wash her right in the crick; the water's warm. I'll wash all of you."

"No, you won't," said the elder sister with decision. "Ma says the dust sticks to us worse if we get too clean. But we can wash Twinkle, if you want to; she won't care."

"I'm going to dress her up, too," announced Joan. "I don't think she ought to go around so skin-out, even on the prairie."

"Have youse got more clothes in the house?" inquired Crystal, with awe.

"We got *some*."

"Gee, you must be awful rich!"

"We ain't rich, but we ain't *starving.*"

"But you got carpets in your house."

"Those old rugs!" said Joan with scorn. "We had nicer things in Platteville. We just brought our for-common out here. And if you think our house is nice you ought to see some of the others back home."

"What did *they* have?"

"Oh, carpets that your feet sink into. And grand pianos and chandeliers. An' fountains in the yard and silver name plates on the door."

Crystal sighed. "Ain't it queer how some folks have things and some folks ain't got any! I should think God'd divide 'em up."

"I asked Uncle Jim about that, once. He said that God proba'ly intended folks to do that, but that there wasn't many of them that had ever learned division. They got as far as multiplication, and then stopped. Now I'll go in and get the things for Twinkle, and don't you girls unpin her till I come back. She's *my* child, we're pertending, and I want the fun of taking off her dress. Pertend I was afraid to trust you with her."

"The Wubbers are here," she called to Becky as she went in the front door. Becky was in the kitchen, and the partition between the rooms hid Joan's half-guilty face.

"That's nice; I'm glad you have some one to play with. Don't hold that baby on your lap; she's too dirty."

"No, I won't. May I have a little soap to wash her face?"

"Of course. But don't get it into her eyes."

Joan hurried out of the door, and Becky, sprinkling clothes at the kitchen table, smiled a little grimly to herself. "Prairie dirt is a little too much for even Joan," she thought. "I could never have let her play with those Wubbers six months ago, but I'm getting more charitable since I'm a homesteader myself. Easy enough to keep clean when you can get water by turning a faucet; but well to pail, pail to kettle, and kettle to wash tub is another story. I don't wonder Mrs. Wubber lies back on the job. It's Fate that her children should all be blondes."

Out under the sun the adopted mother unpinned Twinkle from her one garment, found a shallow place in the creek, and set the baby in the water. Flattered at being the center of attention, she graciously permitted herself to be lathered and scrubbed. Beneath the veneer of dirt appeared fair, rosy cheeks and a clean skin.

"I'm going to do her hair," said Joan, enthusiastic over her charge's changed appearance. "Shut your eyes, baby dear, and let Joan put the nice soap on your head."

But Twinkle had had enough of beauty parlors. The unaccustomed cleanliness disturbed her, and she wriggled her fat body away from the soap, and began to cry. Joan, fearful that the noise would bring Becky to the scene of action, was forced to stop.

"Well, it's better than it was, anyway. I got *some* of the dirt out; you can tell that by the black streams running down her. I'll just have to leave the rest of the soap in; she'll get it in her eyes if I rinse her."

She lifted the soft, baby flesh out of the water and seated Twinkle on the hot earth above the creek bed.

"Look out," warned Venus; "she might fall headwards back."

And that is just what Twinkle did. The edge of the bank crumbled with her weight, and she went down, head first. Joan and Crystal caught her, but not until her wet, soapy head had rolled through the wet, muddy earth.

"Good thing the soap's in it," said Joan. "That'll kinda eat up the dirt. Come, Twinkle, Joan'll put you up on the nice rock. Wish we had a towel, but the sun's so hot it'll dry her quick."

The tender flesh had already begun to turn red in the sunshine. Joan pulled over the baby legs a pair of her own black sateen bloomers, put on a pair of Indian moccasins, and added the blouse of a khaki middy suit. The child looked like a picture from Hans Brinker. The wet hair began to dry, leaving a halo of stiff little wisps.

"I ain't just satisfied with her hair," admitted Joan. "Maybe we could wash it again."

"No, she'll never stand for that."

"Then I'm going to give her a dry shampoo

to make it stand out fluffy.   I'll get some powder to rub on it if Becky lets me."

"Twinkle might blow up."

"Hoh, it's talcum powder, not gun.   Maybe I'd better not ask about the powder; Becky might say no.   Starch'll do just as well."

The victim received a liberal application of starch, which was thoroughly rubbed into her sticky head.   Somehow it didn't seem to make her fluffy.   But the hair was still wet; when it dried, the powder shampoo might be more effectual.

"Le's take her over an' show your mother," suggested Joan.   "I'll go part way with you.   It'll proba'ly 'set' on the way."

"We don't haf to go yet," objected Crystal. "We ain't fit."

Joan was not anxious to have Becky or Dick see the result of her morning's work.   "Well, we might, any time," she predicted.   "You'd better go before we do.   I'll pull her across the draw for you.   Don't she look cute?"

"She's awful red."

The baby's wrists and neck did look scarlet,

SPENT WITH HEAT AND PAIN AND THIRST AND LONELINESS

much redder than she had been when she arrived; and when the children touched her she cringed away from them. She even cried a little when the wagon jolted.

"She acts sick," said Crystal. "Maybe it's the washing; she ain't used to so much rubbing."

"I guess I'd better be going back," said Joan, as they reached the draw. "I guess maybe your mother's too busy hoeing to want me around."

"You better come on an' tell ma that it was you that did it," suggested Crystal.

But the prospect did not sound inviting. "Some other day," said Joan, and she turned and went back over the prairie, leaving the explanation to the Wubbers.

"Where are your friends?" asked Dick, as she passed him in the potato field.

"They hatto go," answered Joan.

THE potatoes were doing well. Their leaves were sturdy and green, and they had begun to bud. Back of the plot in which he was working the corn was high enough to show a ripple when the wind blew through it. The tomatoes were lusty, the cucumbers had sent out their first curly tendrils, and the melons had begun to vine. When Dick was called in to dinner he carried a surprise with him. "Guess what I've got!" he said to Becky, at the kitchen door.

"Another snake?"

"Better than that." He opened his hands to show the first fruit of the garden — ten small red radishes.

Becky gave a squeal of delight. "Oh, Dick, won't they taste heavenly! Where did they come from? I thought the rabbits got every one of our two plantings."

"I tried a third, and sprinkled a little red pepper above each hole. They're pretty small, still, but I was afraid that a rain might wash the pepper away, and the rabbits might get these before we did." He rinsed them in a cup of water, and set them, still dripping, on the table.

"Gee, *radishes!*" said Joan, coming in the door. "I could eat them all at one mouthful. How soon will the rest be ripe?"

"In a day or two, if the rabbits let them alone."

"I can hardly wait. I'm so sick of cans I

never want to see one again. It seemed grand, when we first came out here, to see those long rows of tins, but that was before I had to eat a million of them. The pictures on the outside look so different from the taste inside."

"You ought to have to cook from them," said Becky, sitting down at the table. "That's worse than eating from them. No matter how I season them the tinny taste is always there. Ten radishes: two for you and me, Dick, and three for the kids."

"Two and a half for each one of us," said Joan. "Uncle Jim would have made us divide them even."

Becky gravely cut two of the larger radishes into halves. "Where *is* Phil?"

"He and Autie went to find ground cherries."

"How long ago?"

"Just after the Wubbers came."

"That was two hours ago. I don't like to have him wandering around the prairie that way. He ought to show up for meals, at least."

"He'd be on hand if he knew about the radishes," said Joan.

"I'll save his," said Becky. "He'll be back as soon as he gets hungry."

Dick went back to the garden, and Becky and Joan to the dish washing, but Phil didn't appear. Becky weeded the onion bed, and trained the morning glory vines that had begun to climb around the front door, but her eyes went frequently to the prairie trail. At two he hadn't appeared. At two-thirty she carried the milk and the butter, which had been awaiting him, back to the well, and lowered them into the coolness. At three she went out to Dick, who was hoeing corn in the garden.

"I'm worried about Phil," she said.

"Hasn't that little rat turned up yet?"

"No, and I can't see him from the big hill. I climbed it to look. There's not a sign of him along the creek."

"Maybe he went to the Wubber's with Autie."

"He would have been back by this time."

Dick picked up the spading fork and the hoe with an anxious look on his tanned face. He certainly had grown older, much older, in the months since Uncle Jim died. The careful way in which he cleaned his tools, the worried expression with which he received Becky's announcement, the readiness with which he accepted responsibility was not like the Dick of three months ago. It was a comfort to have him sharing the things that threatened, and the girl felt a nearness that seemed to cut out the two years between their ages.

"I'd better ride over to the Wubber's and see," he said.

He galloped over the prairie, but was back in a few minutes. "They haven't been around there," he reported. "Wubber isn't home, and Mrs. Wubber doesn't seem worried. She's rocking on her stoop. 'He'll show up before long,' she told me, 'Autie always *does* show up.' But I don't want to wait for that. I think I'll start out and round 'em up. Phil has never gone away like this before."

THE two little boys had followed the trail that led between the Linville house and the Welp shack. They found some ground cherries, growing along some furrows that had evidently been the fireguard of some homesteader, and they turned back the papery husks and ate their fill. In Platteville Phil would have scorned their queer, musky taste, but to the fruit-hungry lips of the boys they seemed delicious. Then they had walked a mile to see "The Lone Tree," a single, large cottonwood, that had, by some miracle, been seeded and grown along the trail. It was the first real tree that Phil had seen in Tripp County, and after pounding the ground around it to dislodge any chance snake, the boys lay down under it, and reveled in its shade. The soft grasses waved around them, the gophers popped in and out of their holes, and the meadow-larks whirred close above them.

"Le's go up to the water-mark," suggested Autie.

"What's the water-mark?"

"Haven't you seen those piles of stone built on the hills above the creek? The Indians left them. They built 'em to show where there was water."

"Do you know where is one?"

"Up there. Just on the aige of the hill. You can see it if you look clost."

Phil "looked clost." On the butte above them he could make out a little tower of stones, which he never before had noticed. Together the two boys climbed to the top, and stood panting on the edge of the ravine. The water-mark was made of a circle of big stones, piled one on another, until it was a tower several feet high. Buried in the ground near it Phil found an Indian arrow-head. "This proba'ly was their regular stamping ground," he said. "I wouldn't be surprised if they had many a war dance up here."

Autie agreed. He was the easy-going son of his easy-going mother, and his mild acquiescence was refreshing after two months of constant association with Joan.

"I'll bet they had lots of fights here."

"Sure," agreed Autie, "The Sioux is the worst fighters of all. The prairie is just thick with their arrow-heads. My father turned up nine when he was plowing our east forty."

"Le's go down the hill where the wind don't blow so wild," suggested Phil.

Again Autie agreed, and the boys climbed

down the slope to the little rocky shelf which
jutted out a dozen feet below. Here they sat,
side by side, sheltered from the wind, looking
down at the rolling grass below them. They were
higher than the hawks that sailed lazily above
the prairie; so high that they seemed almost on a
level with the two purple peaks of Dog Ear
Buttes, miles away.

Suddenly something whizzed over their heads.
Both boys looked up just in time to see a noose of
rope poise itself for a second above each one of
them, then tighten around their arms. They felt
themselves being lifted in the air, and pulled several feet above the rocky ledge where they had
been sitting. They looked again, half expecting
a joke, but there was nothing to be seen but the two
stout ropes which hung from the top of the bluff.
The pulling stopped, and the boys hung sus-
pended in the air. They could feel the rope
jerk and give; then finally stop, as though the
mysterious lassoer had fastened the other end.
They struggled to loosen their arms, but the ropes
pulled tighter with each movement. Three feet
above the ledge they dangled, perilously near the

stony face of the butte. Both shouted desper-
ately. There was not a sound in reply except
the whiff, whiff of the wind blowing over their
heads, and the call of the larks in the grass below.

"Do you s'pose it's Indians?" said Phil.

Autie did not answer. He only sobbed.

The sun shone into their eyes, giant grasshoppers jumped into their faces, and hungry flies settled on them. Autie, who hung nearer the hillside, and had one hand free, kicked his legs until
he swung back and forth, and tried to pull himself to the face of the bluff. But the grass broke
in his grasp, and there was nothing else within
reach. It seemed impossible that they should
be stranded there. They were so near safety, and
yet they were unable to reach it. They shrieked
again and again, but nobody answered. The
wind whistled overhead, and the sun beat down.

Before they had hung an hour it seemed like a
whole day. When two hours had dragged themselves away it was like a year. As the sun went
farther west the butte failed to shadow them;
they were exposed to a glare and heat that was
almost unbearable. Sometimes the boys called;

sometimes they cried; sometimes they struggled. In one of his mad attempts to reach the hillside and pull himself to safety Autie struck his head upon a jutting rock which cut a gash over one eye. The blood ran down his face and stiffened his overalls, making a feast for every fly in the neighborhood, and there seemed to be hundreds of them. The children did their best to help each other — Phil trying in vain to get a handkerchief out of his pocket for Autie's wound, and Autie struggling, with his one free arm, to keep the flies off both of them.

"Becky'll be looking for us," comforted Phil. "She'll get Dick out after us."

"My folks won't even know I'm gone," moaned Autie.

"Dick'll take *you* home, too." There was a pause filled only with the buzzing of flies and the call of a far-off mourning dove. "If he can see us, way up here," Phil added.

There came a time when it seemed as though the ropes must cut them in two at the waist; when a belt of numbness circled each body, and their feet and hands seemed going to sleep. Then it was that they stopped crying and struggling and hung limply, spent with heat and pain and thirst and loneliness. Their eyes had ceased to search the prairie below. They did not see Dick who rode across the waves of grass below, calling and looking everywhere.

It was Autie's tow head, a white spot against the green, that caught Dick's attention. He strained his eyes to see. What was it that made the two specks of color on the hillside? He turned Job off the slough grass and toward the butte. It took ages for the horse to wind his way up the stony incline. Dick's heart went into his mouth as he climbed till the ropes came into view. Had those two boys hanged themselves in play? Was this what the prairies had done to the Linvilles? He gave a great cry. The boys heard it and opened their eyes. Back to Dick, borne on the breeze, came a faint halloo.

"Alive, alive!" sang Dick's heart. He urged Job on as far as the horse could go up the hill. Then he dismounted, and climbed the last and steepest part of the slope. He stood on the ledge, caught each boy in an arm, and eased the strain of the cruel ropes. It was only a moment before both bonds were cut, the children were laid side by side on the ledge, and Dick was rubbing their lame bodies to restore the circulation.

"I knew you'd find me," said Phil's parched lips.

While the two children lay resting on the grass Dick left them and climbed to the summit of the hill to reconnoitre. There was not a sign of anyone near; not a footprint that the boy could find. But the ropes still hung from the edge of the cliff, weighted down by great stones from the water-mark. He stooped down, and pulled one of the lassoes toward him. It was made of a new piece of twisted hemp, and at the end was a halter snap.

"That," exclaimed Dick, "is the rope that fastened Red Haw."

The shadows had begun to lengthen when Job with his triple burden came down the trail. Autumn, who was the first to recover from his experience, was able to sit up behind Dick, but Phil still leaned limply against his brother. Becky and Joan met them a quarter mile from home.

They had been hunting along the creek bed till they were discouraged and frightened. It was like heaven to see Job ambling down the dusty road, carrying the three boys. Becky only delayed them for a fragmentary story; then hurried the rescue party on to the house. The two girls followed, plowing through the prairie grass, holding hands tightly, and squeezing each other now and then in relief and joy. As they hurried through the door they caught sight of the morning glory vines which an hour before had reached their green tendrils half way up the sides of the door. Now they lay, a tangle of string and withered leaves, on the ground, their roots torn from the ground.

"The Welp boys have been here," said Joan.

Becky's relief at having Phil back again was swept up by a great wave of fear. There was no getting away from an enemy like that. Spite and hatred seemed to envelop them on all sides. Where would it strike next?

It was twenty minutes later that Dick lifted Autie on the horse to take him home. Becky had washed and dressed his wound, and put on a clean suit of overalls that belonged to Phil. The boy seemed cheerful, and, except for his cut, not much the worse for his bad afternoon.

"I suppose your mother will be worried to death about you," said Dick, as they loped over the prairie trail.

"Ma ain't the worrying kind," was the reply.

And Autie evidently knew his mother. As they drove up, at six-thirty, Mrs. Wubber sat just where she had been sitting three hours before. She was still rocking. She looked as though she had rocked since morning. Dick told the story of the outrage, starting with indignation, and ending with almost fury, but Mrs. Wubber did not seem greatly disturbed. She rocked and listened and rocked. "I always knew those Welp boys were mean cusses," was her only comment. When Dick unfastened Autie's bandage and exposed the jagged cut, he expected an outburst of anxiety and wrath, but nothing of the kind was forthcoming.

"All my kids is got scars now," she remarked with what seemed like satisfaction.

"This has been a day of worry for you," said Dick, as he mounted Job to go back home.

"That cut won't last long on Autie," she said. "He's a quick healer. But Twinkle, now, she got a worse deal. I guess there's no way but I got to wash her head tomorrow."

CHAPTER VII

A MESSAGE FROM UNCLE JIM

THE golden days of June became the molten days of July. The sky was cloudless and the sun was a blinding glare. The winds that stirred the air were hotter than the air itself and seemed to be blown across a fiery furnace. The meadow-larks were silent, and the gardens on the breaking withered.

Three weeks of the blazing sunshine. The green carpet that had unrolled before them two months ago disappeared, and a dry mat of slippery hay covered the earth. The corn was no longer shiny and green; the blades were pale yellow and crinkled with heat. Nobody said, any more, that it was good corn weather. At first they had complained that it was too dry; then they had said that they *must* get rain; now they had stopped talking about it. The few homesteaders that drove by on the trail were so discouraged and blue that they frequently didn't rein up their horses at all as they passed by.

Becky and Dick made a brave fight to save the garden. They shielded the sickly plants from the sun with cloths and tin cans; they hoed the earth around and around the roots; they carried pail after pail of water to the clearing. But the tendrils of the cucumbers burned away, the melon vines were seared, and the tomatoes hung their limp heads. One by one the leaves on the two transplanted trees turned yellow, withered, blew away. Even Castor and Pollux looked ready to die, though each day Becky loosened the dirt around their roots, and each night she carried water from the creek to pour around them.

"I just can't bear to lose them," she said. "They're the only green thing I can see from the window."

"Wish we'd had a picture taken of the claim before everything dried up," said Joan. "Our place looks almost as bad as the Welpses, now. If we had a contest there wouldn't be anything to show for all that work we did."

"I'd just as soon the Welps *would* get the land, if this is the kind of summers they have in Tripp County. I don't think this is much of a place to live," growled Phil.

The children no longer sought their old haunts. It was too hot to play near the little homestead; the prairie dog town blazed under the fierce sun; the creek was drying up. The last time they had played there water stood only in the deeper pools, and in one of the shallower basins Phil had counted twelve small striped snakes wriggling over one another in a vain attempt to get beneath the water. It was too hot to play; too hot to work. The children hung about in the shadow cast by the barn, listlessly trying and discarding schemes for comfort, and quarreling with each other. Becky's nerves, already frayed by the heat, were more and more worn by the discord. The tiny kitchen was almost unbearable in the middle part of the day, and out of it came nothing that was appetizing. Bacon and ham and dried beef, canned vegetables, last year's potatoes that were almost too limber to pare, butter that melted while it was being carried on the table, fried eggs, beans, dried fruit and milk was their fare, day after day. The children's appetites began to wane.

There was no prospect of change in their menu. For weeks they had been living in hope of that garden, watching each green head poke its way through the earth, rejoicing in each inch of growth. "Perhaps in a week the beans will be ready; by August we may be able to dig our first early potatoes." But there was no chance of that now; no future of fruit or vegetables to look forward to. Unless they had rain now, at once, the garden was doomed. And there was no rain in sight. There was never a cloud in the sky, the sun held its shining course day after day, and the dry wind blew and blew and blew. Becky closed her ears with her hands, sometimes, to shut out the sound.

On one of the hottest of these July days Dick was out in the garden. There was no further need of stirring the soil; what was turned up was as dry as the surface. He walked about through the yellowing rows, and with sinking heart looked at the ruin of his summer's work. The potatoes had been the last to yield to the drought. They had flowered abundantly, and Dick and Becky had rejoiced over the prospect of a full crop. With milk and potatoes one could live, even if other things failed. Today he took the spading fork and turned up the dry earth around one of the plants. No potatoes. He dug around another: not a tuber there, either. He dug up a third and fourth. At the roots of the fifth he found one tiny potato, the size of an acorn.

Two horseback riders crossed the creek, and came picking their way along the dusty trail. As they rounded the potato patch they gave a derisive "hi there!" and Dick looked up to see the grinning faces of the two Welp boys.

"Fine potato crop you got," remarked Pete.

Dick made no reply, but went on digging.

"Don't worry over 'em; those are our spuds, not

yours. Paw filed a contest on you yesterday."
And they rode on laughing.

The dry dust from the potato field blew into
Dick's face as he looked down the trail at their
retreating backs. He hoped Becky had not
heard their remark. She would have to know
about the contest, of course, but this was no time
to tell her — while this blight lay upon the
earth. She had enough to worry about now.

He turned on his heel and went into the house.
Becky was setting the table in the sitting-room
to get away from the oven-like air of the kitchen.
Her face looked worn and her eyes stare-y.

"I saw you digging the early potatoes," she
said.

Dick made no response.

"Well?" inquired Becky.

"Not a potato on them."

"You sure?"

"Dead sure."

Becky went on laying the knives and forks at
each place. "Would a rain save anything in
the garden?"

"Not unless it came tonight. The melons are

burnt up, and the tomatoes almost gone. Some of them are burned off at the roots. I did hope we were going to have some potatoes, but I'm afraid they're doomed. Rain might save the cabbage plants, and give the turnips a start, but there's no hope of rain. Look at that sky!"

Becky did not look at the sky; she did not look at her brother. Her eyes faced despair. "What are we going to do?" she asked.

Dick did not answer. Becky went on: "Uncle Jim figured that we could get through the winter if we had fodder and potatoes. If we don't have them how can we make it? With the Glovers behind in their rent there'll be no money for even groceries."

Her brother leaned his head on the beam that ran alongside the window, and looked out into the blinding sunshine. He stood still, without a reply, as Becky went back and forth from hot sitting-room to hotter kitchen.

The children came in languidly at her summons to the meal, and Becky turned out the oil stove and followed them. She had tried to vary the monotonous menu by a little baking, and with her face flushed with the heat, she set a plate of smoking cornbread on the table. Nobody touched it. Dick drank his milk, Phil indifferently accepted a hard-boiled egg, Joan took an empty plate. Becky's face hardened as she looked round the table.

"I'd like to know what's the use of baking myself over that stove if nobody's going to eat!" she exclaimed angrily.

The children looked up amazed. Was this from serene Becky, this overwrought, petulant voice and angry inflection?

"You needn't be so sore," said Dick. "I can't eat that cornbread without butter, and I don't like butter when it swims in the dish."

"Well, I didn't melt it!" snapped Becky.

"Gee, but you're cranky," commented Phil. "Scolding us for not being hungry. And I don't see as you're taking anything, yourself."

"Things look so awful uneatish out here," complained Joan. "Just think what we'd be having in Platteville now — black raspberries, and big red tomatoes sliced on lettuce, and crispy little radishes — "

"And ice-cold watermelons," put in Phil.

"And cherries and big, red plums — "

"And green apple sauce and frozen custard and new potatoes — "

"Be still!" said Dick savagely.

They finished the meal in silence. The children wiped the dishes, and Dick put a saddle on Job.

"Where you going?" asked Phil.

"Winner," answered Dick. "I'll be back for supper." Becky heard him go to the pocketbook in the bureau drawer. "Do you want anything?"

"A lot of things there's no money for." She watched him take out one of the bills. "We can't spare a cent of that," she said sharply.

"Whose money *is* it?" inquired Dick with spirit. He went out with the money, and the screen door slammed behind him.

The grasshoppers flew up in swarms as Job trotted slowly over the trail to Winner. At the Wubber gate his driver stopped to speak to the tow-headed family that flowed over the chicken-wire gate to meet him. The Wubber cornstalks, yellow and dry, rustled in the hot wind.

"How are things?" called Dick.

Mr. Wubber shook his head. "Bad."

"How's your corn?"

"Dry enough to pop, if it had any ears on it. Ain't goin' to git a thing out of the year's work. The Missus says she's fed up with homesteading."

Dick's eyes followed the indicating thumb. There, in the open door of the hen house, sat the rocking-chair with Mrs. Wubber inside of it. Under that low-roofed shack the heat must have been terrific, but she was reading a torn paper-backed novel, and fanning herself with a news-paper as she rocked.

"Been out there most of the day," explained Mr. Wubber. "When the wind's from this way it rattles the corgerated iron roof on the house till it makes her crazy. She says she can't stand the banging. That's why she sets out there."

"Maybe it'll blow up a storm," said Dick.

"No hope for that," replied Mr. Wubber. "No weather-breeder about that breeze — it's

straight prairie wind.   Myself, I don't mind it,
but it gits the women folks."

Dick thought over the speech as he urged Job
along the prairie trail.   Was that what was the
matter with Becky, that made her so jerky and
irritable?   She hadn't looked right lately, and
she jumped if anyone dropped a cup or the door
banged.   Did the wind "git" her, or was it the
worry?   Poor Beck!   They were all having a
hard enough time, but she was getting the tough-
est end of it.   He wished he had not slammed the
screen door.   Well, he knew what he must do —

FROM noon to three o'clock was the hottest part
of the day.   Becky ironed in the sitting-room,
with her board placed between the doors to catch
the breeze that stirred, but did not cool, the air.
Birds sat motionless on the barbed wire fence,
in the tiny shade cast by the posts, and the air
seemed to dance as she looked out over the dry
prairie.   Perspiration drenched the blue gingham apron, and her head felt dizzy and too large
for her body, but the basket of ironing was almost
emptied.   "No use in leaving it for another day;

no hope of tomorrow's being any cooler." She was on Dick's last blue shirt when the children burst in at the door, both crying.

"It's wrecked. It's all broken up!" Becky made out between sobs.

"What's broken, children?"

"Oh, our homestead. Our little claim! The buildings are all smashed — "

"And the windmill — "

"It's all torn up."

She followed them down to the bank of the dry creek. It looked as though a tornado had struck the site of the little homestead. The farm buildings were split in pieces, the wheels were wrenched off the carts, the fragments of the windmill lay in the creek bottom. Nothing had been spared. The plaything was a wreck.

"It was those Welp boys! I know it was those Welp boys!" exclaimed Phil, his voice shrill with fury and excitement. "I saw Bill and Pete ridin' along the creek this noon. They must have seen my little farm and smashed it while we were all in the house. Oh, Becky, my farm!"

Becky tried to comfort the little fellow. "I'll

help you build another," she said, with her arms around him.

"I can't build another; that was the last of the boxes."

"I'd just like to catch those ole sneaks," scolded Joan. "They waited around here till they knew Bronx and Dick were gone. I'd like to tie wasps' nests to 'em."

"Can't we do something to them, Becky? Have them arrested or something? I'm afraid they'll kill us if they get the chance."

Becky laughed at the fear, but it was not a genuine laugh. The same thought had threatened her when the two little boys were found strung up on the hillside, and had never left her since. Broken windows, loosened stock, torn-up flowers and smashed toys could be endured, but would the Welp family stop at depredations? Becky hugged her little brother tightly. How long would the children be safe?

She comforted them with the promise of more box lumber and her help in building.

"Why don't you pull two washtubs up in front of the shack and fill them with water?" she suggested. "It'll begin to be shady there before long. Put on your worst clothes and you can have a good time splashing around. It will cool you off, anyway."

Phil and Joan forgot their grief in their delight at the idea, as they ran in for overalls and out again for tubs. Becky looked at the thermometer which hung at the door. "Hundred and three in the shade," she said; "if there is any shade to *be* in." She put away the ironing board and the smooth stack of linen, and took Uncle Jim's old sweater from her pile of mending. "Dick will be wanting this some day," she thought; "If it ever gets cool enough to wear a sweater!"

But she did not sew. She sat with the needle in her hand, and looked out at the dry world that lay beyond. The prairie seemed to be rolling in on them instead of away from them; it was like a threatening enemy, not a welcoming friend. Only a month ago it had invited them, holding out its green lap of plenty; now it had turned a traitorous face. They could never hope to make friends with it.

The hot wind sucked in at the south door and out at the north. It flapped the awning; it pounded the screen door. The strips of black cloth tacked on to the outside to keep away the flies snapped in the breeze till the edges were frayed. The gusts of hot air rose and fell like waves of the sea, with a noise that waxed and waned, but never stopped. Becky remembered Mrs. Kenniker on the wind: "It nags at you and nags at you and nags at you till it finally gets you." . . . Was that what was the matter with *her?* Was it the worry over the drought and fear of the Welp family that was making her nervous, or was it the prairie wind? She had not been sleeping well since the hot weather set in, and she was not hungry either; nothing tasted good out of cans.

Perhaps what Phil had said about her at noon was true: Yes, she had been cranky lately; she could recall more than one irritable speech. But that wasn't *her* fault; she was not naturally a cross person: it must be the wind; if it would only stop its eternal nagging she could stand all the rest of the discomforts. . . But how she hated the heat and the flies! How she despised the dirt!

How she missed the sink, and dreaded the carrying and emptying water. How she rebelled at
the traces of the barnyard that seemed ever-pres-
ent, and how she longed for the old bathroom at
home! She could get along without companionship; she could give up school; she didn't mind
the hard work or the loneliness. But it was
the daintiness she missed, and it was impossible
to be dainty on the Dakota prairie when it was
a hundred and three by the thermometer.

She laid her hot face down on the table beside
Uncle Jim's sweater. It brought back Uncle
Jim so vividly, with its smell of tobacco and that
tear in the pocket — the pocket that he had
caught on the kitchen cabinet the last time he
wiped dishes for her. Oh, if Uncle Jim were
only there, to advise, to plan, and to comfort! If
he were with them they wouldn't fail in homesteading; he would find a way out. She picked
up the needle and took the sweater off the table.
Out of the pocket a little shower dropped into
her lap: Uncle Jim's knife was there, a black
button from his vest, three matches, one of the
little, smooth, shiny stones that he was always

picking up. And besides this tiny hoard of treasures was a small blank book, with a four-leafed clover pressed between its pages. There were figures on most of its sheets, and memoranda of various kinds in his neat handwriting. And on the fourth page she found this:

> *Enter on check book*
> *$ 6.80 flour*
> *$15.00 potatoes*
> *$25.00 church*
> *$12.25 school books*
>
> *Call up Gronau*
> *See about winter's coal*
> *Cout's Life of Napoleon*
> *Taxes*
> *Joan's muff*
>
> *The road to a mountain top is always a*
> *zig-zag one. Sit tight.*

The tears rushed to her eyes. Uncle Jim came back with the words. The prairie shack melted away into space, and she was back in the Platteville living-room. And he was near her, standing with his hands in the pockets of that old gray sweater, looking down at her with the smile wrinkles about his eyes. No matter whether those words were a quotation, or his own, no matter why he had written them in the book, they were his message to her. She could hear him saying them; she could *see* him saying them. He was there *with her*. Oh, Uncle *Jim* . . .

And then the Platteville living-room was gone. She was back in the hot shack, the gray sweater was empty, and the prairie wind was banging the screen door. But the wind was no longer an excuse for irritation and discouragement. She saw how she had been sheltering herself behind it for the past weeks; how she had been trying to fool herself with the idea that it alone was responsible for her ill-humor. "You big baby!" said Becky to herself. *"Pitying yourself!"* No doubt that things were hard and times were discouraging, but you couldn't go down under them. And if you did go down it was your own fault, and not the wind's . . . "Sit tight," Uncle Jim had said. Well, she would.

She stooped down to pick up a piece of paper that had fallen where Joan had changed her dress. On it was written in Joan's unmistakable spelling:

> *Lime*
> *garpe*
> *orange croosh*
> *cheery bloosom*
> *ginger ail*
> *hiry's rote Beir.*

"Poor little kid! *She's* been longing for something cool, too," thought Becky. She jumped up from the chair, and laid the gray sweater back in the mending basket. That could wait. She heated water and bathed, and put on one of the clean dresses she had just ironed. She made cocoa and set it to cool; she mixed a near-salad, of gelatine and tomato juice, opened a bottle of olives and made floating island. She hung everything down the well to chill them. She spread sandwiches of thin bread and butter, and then she called the children and made them clean for the meal. Somehow the heat didn't seem so unbearable after clothes were changed. She and the children milked the cow, watered the horse, and fed the chickens, and the chores were done and the meal ready when Dick came slowly back over the trail from Winner. He was whistling as he drove up to the door.

"Any supper for a hard-working man?" he called. "Got something for you." And he laid down in front of Becky a letter from Aunt Jule.

"What you got in that bundle?" demanded the children, as the older lad deposited a bulging paper sack on the kitchen table.

"Never you mind. Business before pleasure; let's have the letter: It's a peach. I read it."

Dear Children:

I fell in front of Sander's gate, on his broken sidewalk which should have been mended months ago, and sprained my wrist three weeks ago so haven't been able to write. I have my arm out of the sling now, and it is still very painful, but I feel that I ought to make the effort to write you even if you children don't feel obligated to write me. I have never heard one word from you except Becky's two letters and Joan's postcard.

We are having very warm weather here, and the crops need rain. I see by the papers that this is a bad season in Tripp County, and that you are due for a complete failure. I never had the faith in that country that Jim had. I hope you are not going to lose everything, but if you children did the planting I don't suppose you had much to lose.

Your house looks pretty run down. The Glovers seem to be dirty, easy-going tenants, and don't keep things up the way they should. They have cut down the hard maple that Jim planted, and I notice that two of the windows are broken. I don't suppose they will keep the place long. I hope they will stay, for you'll need the money before the year is out. I worry about you often, and wonder how you are getting along. I suppose you are all out at the elbows.

The M. E. church cleared $18.90 on their chicken dinner last week. They expected more. Mrs. Hunter is down with rheumatism, and

Grandpa Patterson has had a stroke and is unconscious.

Did you take your walnut book shelves with you? If they are stored here in Platteville I could use them, and save you the price of storage. Let me hear from you at once.

Your affectionate aunt,

Juliet McGrudy

Becky laughed her first real laugh for weeks.

"Cheery, isn't it?" said Dick, seating himself at the table. "Gee, this has been a hot day! This cold cocoa tastes great, Beck. Well, I have two pieces of good news for you: The first is that I dropped Aunt Jule a postcard saying she might use the bookcase. It's too wide to get through any door in her house, as she'll find after she's paid the drayman to bring it up."

"Dick!"

"Why not? Your cry was always not to argue with her. Nothing else I could write her would ever convince her that the shelves were too big for her house."

Becky looked amused, but worried. "I don't like to make trouble for Aunt Jule — " she began.

"I do," said Joan, eating her floating island with relish. "What's the other good news, Dick?"

"Well, I went into Mr. Cleaver's office, and asked him if he knew where I could get a job in the fall. I told him that things looked bad out here, and that we'd have a slim chance of scraping through the winter if I couldn't earn something to help. He told me that he didn't see what I could do — that there were a dozen homesteaders to every job in Tripp county. But he suggested something for you, Beck."

"Me? What could I do?"

"He says he thinks you could get a school if you went after it. Seems that the people who settled this district first are crazy for a teacher for their kids. They tried to get one last year, and couldn't find a soul. He asked me how much schooling you had had, and when I told him that you were all ready for normal school he said that he felt sure that you could get a job somewhere. He knows the School Commissioner well, and said he'd ask for the place in this district if you wanted it."

Becky looked overjoyed, then dubious. "But I never taught school a day in my life!"

"That's what I told him. But he said there were many teachers out in this part of the country with just half your preparation. The people want schools so much that they'll take girls of sixteen without any training at all."

"But who'd do our cooking if you were teaching?" inquired Joan.

"We'd all have to hop to and help," said Dick. "If Becky's going to support us we've got to board her."

"Where could I hold school? Here in the house?"

"No, he says there's a school building two miles and a half west of here, in Crane Hollow. It was built last year, but never used because they couldn't find a teacher."

"It's too good to be true. I can't believe that I'd ever get it."

"He said you were to let him know, right away, if you wanted it, and he'd go after the place for you.   Said you could probably make forty-five dollars a month."

"But Dick, *arithmetic!*"

"Well, I mentioned that you always counted dots on your paper when you were adding, and he said to tell you to stop doing it in front of people.   Said you were the smartest girl he'd seen among the homesteaders — he evidently doesn't know many of them! — and that if he had children he'd be tickled to have you teaching them."

Becky's eyes shone.

"He said not to mention our plans, because old man Welp would probably do all he could to keep you from getting the school. "

"Did you tell him about the lassoing?"

"I did, and he was as hot as I was.   Said that the worst thing about it was that we were so helpless with a man like Welp; if we had him bound over to keep the peace he'd probably burn the shack down at night, or do something equally lawless.   The only thing to do was to keep away from them; not even let the children go where they'd be *likely* to have a run-in with them.   If the

Welps got too lawless, he said, the homesteaders themselves would step in and force them out of the county, which of course would be the best thing in the world for us. He advised us to mind our own business, never to speak to them, and if they threatened us again to let him know. Mr. Cleaver's a peach, Beck."

"It's wonderful to have him to go to for advice."

"I told him that, and he laughed and said it was wonderful to find anybody who *wanted* advice these days; that it was far more blessed to give than to receive."

"I hope he doesn't feel that the Linvilles are hanging on him too much."

"He didn't act as though he did. He kept me in his office a long time, and asked all about the corn and the potatoes and what improvements we had made, and if we were lonesome, and how you were standing it — "

"What did you tell him about that?"

Dick looked mischievous. "I told him that I thought the wind was making you a bit edgy; that your practically perfect disposition seemed frazzled lately. And he said, 'When she feels that way pack her up and bring her in to Dallas to my wife; she'll sympathize with her. When I first brought Mrs. Cleaver out here from Ohio she said the wind used to blow her spirits out just like electric fuses.' "

"I'm not afraid of the wind now. Oh, Dick, everything will be smooth sailing if I get that school!"

"Look what I brought home!" said Dick. He opened the paper bag that the children had been eyeing, and thrust it under the three noses in succession.

"Oranges!" exclaimed Joan and Phil.

"Lemons!" said Becky.

"Let's lie in the lap of luxury," proposed Dick. "Beck, you squeeze the lemons; Phil, you get the big pitcher; Joan, you bring the sugar. In the meantime, I'll see if I can't manage to scurry around and dip out the water! We'll drink to Becky's school in real lemonade."

CHAPTER VIII

PRAIRIE BONDS

'S YOUR turn to feed the chickens," said Joan to Phil.

" 'Tis not. It's yours."

"Phil Linville, don't you remember that I took the scraps out early this morning, an' that ole rooster snipped me in the arm?"

"That was yestiddy."

"It was not. Look at the mark! Does that look like a yestiddy scar?"

"Gee, you're always trying to get out of work,"

said Phil. "I did all the chores this morning —
with Dick."

"Quit your scrapping," called Dick from the
barn. "Trouble with you kids is that you haven't
enough work. You ought to be made to do all
the chores except milking. Then you wouldn't
have so much time to fight."

"Why don't you children carry out the chicken
feed together?" advised Becky. "Then you
could get to playing sooner. I thought you were
going to have a circus this morning."

"We *were* going to have one," said Phil
gloomily. "We had two gophers for it. But
one gnawed his way out of the box last night, an'
we always have a fight because Joan insists on
being the trainer. There's only one that can be
that, and she won't be the audience. That's the
reason I don't like Dakota; there's never any
folks for audiences."

The rain had come at last, but too delayed to do
much good. The late potatoes could be helped,
the parsnips and turnips would be started, but
the corn would amount to nothing, and the gardens had gone beyond saving. There *were* no

crops anywhere, except in the land along the
Keya Paha River, where the homesteaders had
had more rain. Becky had resigned herself to
the absence of green vegetables, and was doing
her best to satisfy the children's craving for fruit
by preserving the few things that grew in that
orchard-less country. The drought had affected
the wild plums, and their fruit was small and
hard, but Becky made them into a jam which the
children welcomed as a change from their
monotonous fare. She bought thriftily of
lemons to flavor the tasteless ground cherries.
And as she dug around the roots of the sickly
currant bushes she dreamed of the jelly she would
have next summer. Surely Dakota wouldn't suf-
fer a drought, next year

Uncle Jim's note-book had given her new cour-
age. She replanted the vines that had been torn
down at the door, and watered the few flowers
that the drought had spared. Castor and Pollux looked like feather dusters, with their long,
naked stems, but their heads were putting out
fresh green leaves, and making two tiny spots
of shade on the dry yard. And it was easier to

be hopeful when the thermometer dropped a
little, and the prairie cooled instead of baked.

Becky thought of Phil's words as she bent over
the only two tomato plants left of the dozens that
they had started, and tied their limpy stalks to
a stake.   That *was* the hard part of homesteading — that you never had an audience.   Trouble
and disappointment you could stand if you could
only talk them over with someone; she could
have laughed at hardships if she had had Mary
Dennison, or some of the other dear Platteville
girls to laugh with her.   If Mr. Cleaver lived
near enough to see occasionally it wouldn't be so
bad.   But there was not only no audience in
Tripp County, but no companionship.   How
could you be intimate with people who weren't
like you, who hadn't a thought in common with
you?   It was hard to be even neighborly with
most of them.   There didn't seem to be much
friendliness on the prairies.

Bronx, who had been lying in the soft dirt
beside her, wrinkled his alert nose, gave a bark,
and bounded wildly over the trail.

"Someone's coming," called Joan.

"Maybe it's the Welps," said Phil with fear in his eyes.

But Bronx came back down the trail with Mrs. Kenniker, her ugly red calico dress swinging against a horse. "The Oleson baby's dead," she announced.

"That curly-headed little thing that lived on the claim near the Lone Tree?"

"That's the one."

"Had she been sick long?"

"Took this morning. Bit by a snake. She was only ailing a few minutes; then she took a spell and died. Wasn't nobody there but her pa and ma. She's all they got, except a big boy."

The children gathered around the gray horse with wonder and sympathy in their faces. They felt a sudden bond with the Oleson family — the sullen-looking man and the sad-faced woman to whom they had nodded when they passed in their wagon.

"He come over fer me," continued Mrs. Kenniker. "He had to drive in to town to get a coffin, and she didn't want to lay out the baby alone.

Ole, the boy, is working down on the Keha Paha, and she's all alone. I promised Oleson I'd go over and help, but I don't like to go alone. I got a dread on me about dead people. I thought I'd drive this way, and get you to mosey along."

Becky began at once to take off her apron. "Dick, will you harness Job for me?" she asked. "Good thing I was up early this morning. The house is clean and the dinner all ready to cook. Dick will finish that, and you two children can wash the dishes afterward. Please don't slop the water all over the clean floor, and *don't* fight while I'm away!"

Mrs. Kenniker smiled a grim smile. "That's one trouble I ain't got," she said. "Marietta ain't got anyone to fight with, and if she had she ain't much on the scrap. The Mister and me does all the rowing at our house."

Becky picked up the reins, added a few last words of instruction, and swung herself into the saddle. The two horses set off over the dusty trail to the Oleson house.

"How you getting along with the Welpses?" asked her companion as they passed in sight of the enemy's rusty stovepipe. "They leaving you be?"

"We haven't found anything wrong for several weeks."

"Then they ain't been around your way, be sure of that. They always leave a piece of cussedness in their trail. I've known a lot of mean folks in my time — I was born of 'em and married with 'em, but I ain't never seen a meaner man than Peter Welp, unless it was his two sons."

"Do they make trouble for you, too?"

"They don't dare do any real damage, 'cause they're scart of Mister. They'd rather try their devilment on a family of children. But those miserable big boys make life terrible for Marietta."

"How?"

"Oh, mocking her, and hunching up a shoulder at her, and calling to know who she's got her back up at. She hates even to go to church fer fear they'll yell after her. I could kill 'em fer that. Marietta's on to her looks without anybody reminding her."

"I think she's a lovely-looking girl. Her eyes

are so clear you can almost look through them."

"Yes, she's got nice eyes, but folks are too busy spotting her crooked back to look at her face. She was born straight enough, but her pa knocked her over one day, when he was drunk. He didn't aim to do it, but he stumbled and fell agin her — she was just starting to walk — and knocked her down. When she could walk again she was crooked that way."

"Couldn't she ever be helped?"

Mrs. Kenniker's horse dropped back a few paces, so her face was out of Becky's sight. "I tried it. The day I first noticed that her back was wrong I took her to a doctor. That was out in Gregory County. He was a good doctor — one of those cancer removers — but he couldn't help her. We paid him in potatoes, and it took our whole crop that year. Finally I seen his treatments weren't doing no good, and then he said she'd have to go to Sioux City fer an operation, and it would cost a hundred and fifty dollars. I began to save fer it that very night. I laid eighteen cents in a tea-box in my pantry as soon as I got home, and whenever I got a little

egg money I'd put a few cents to it. But every-
time I got a little scraped together Marietta'd
be sick, and I'd have to spend it. She was such
a pindling baby that she caught everything that
came along. I had ninety dollars saved the time
she had typhoid, and it all went. After she was
well I began to save again. It took me three
years to get a hundred dollars. Then the Mister
hitched up and we drove into Sioux City with
her. She was at the hospital two weeks."

Mrs. Kenniker stopped talking. Becky
glanced at her. The tight skin seemed to be
stretched tighter than ever across the bones of
the thin face.

"And then what?"

"It was too late," said Mrs. Kenniker dully.
"They said if she'd come three years sooner she
could 'a' been fixed. Git up, Jerry."

The two horses jogged on, side by side, over
the dusty prairie.

"That's why I'm so anxious to get her learned.
She's an awful smart child; ketches on to book-
reading and writing right away. She won't never
be able to do much hard work, and I'd like to

get her learned so she can be a teacher, herself, some day. But we couldn't get a school out here last year. We got the building put up in Crane Hollow, and then the teacher didn't show up. We couldn't get another, and it stood empty all winter. Now we're after the school commissioner hard, and he's promised us one this year."

"Do you know who it's going to be?"

"No, I don't. But I heard yesterday that he had one chose."

Becky's heart sank. That meant that the position she had hoped for was gone.

"There's the Oleson place," said Mrs. Kenniker, pointing ahead of her.

"Place" was the name for it. It wasn't a home; it wasn't even a shack. It was a sod shanty set down in a tiny clearing. Behind it shivered some yellow cornstalks; a gaunt cow and a rusty plow made two spots of shade on the landscape, and some ragged chickens pecked the bare ground. The two visitors picked their way through a dooryard littered with boards and empty barrels. The door casing stood empty, and through the opening they saw an untidy woman sitting on an unmade bed.

She looked up as they entered, but did not leave her seat. She pointed, without a word, to a stretcher on the side of the room — a stretcher made by laying the outside door across two wooden chairs. And on this lay the pitiful little figure they had come to help. Nothing had been done since her death except to lift her from bed to pine door. She lay as she had been carried in, with yellow curls uncombed, and baby fingers stained with soil. She still wore her ugly little brown calico dress. There was no sign of death or disease about her except the one swollen leg that showed where the venom had entered.

Becky looked about her, uncertain where to begin. The sod house was divided into two rooms. One held nothing but a wall bunk, a stool, and an oil stove, with several lard buckets hanging on nails above it. In the other room there was a bed, two wooden chairs, and a baby buggy. A home-made table was pushed against the earth wall, and clothes were hung along the side of the room. There were no carpets, no curtains, no plaster, no floors. The sunlight blazed in through open window and door, chickens pecked the earth floor, and flies buzzed everywhere. Mrs. Kenniker drove the chickens out of the house and barred their entrance with boards, while Becky heated water in the lard pails that seemed to be the only kitchen utensils. Then they washed the little child, and brushed her fair hair. Of linen there was nothing in the house; no sheets, no towels, no clean cloths, even. When they asked for underwear the woman brought out a pair of dark calico bloomers.

"Ain't you got any white cloth in the house?" asked Mrs. Kenniker.

Mrs. Oleson went to a pine box in the room, and produced two flour sacks, with traces of the flour inside. They washed them in a lard pail, and dried them in the hot sunshine. From the two pieces of coarse cloth Mrs. Kenniker fashioned a white slip, which they put on the baby.

"I cut it so she wouldn't have 'Rooster Flour' running acrost her," she whispered.

Becky looked at the dull calico dress, the clumsy bloomers, the dark tan stockings which

BECKY LAID A CLEAN WHITE CLOTH OVER THE PILLOWS

the mother had laid out. "Don't put them on, yet," she whispered to Mrs. Kenniker. "I'll go over home and pick up a few clothes. I'm sure I can find something better for the little thing."

"I can't bear to put that caliker dress on that baby."

"Neither can I."

"Marietta's got a white dress. It's the apple of her eye, but I think she'd give it up. In a case of need, like this now — "

"Don't ask her for it till I see what I have. Do you suppose Mrs. Oleson would be offended if I brought back some clothes?"

"No, I don't," said Mrs. Kenniker, with a glance at the woman who sat gazing straight ahead of her, only looking up when they spoke to her. "She ain't got a thing in the house. Bare cupboards is a good cure for pride."

Together they pulled up the coarse blankets on the bed and plumped up the turkey-red pillows. Then Becky rode back over the trail to get the things that were most sorely needed. She found the house quiet and in order, so she did not disturb the children, whose voices sounded from the thicket, as she packed her basket to carry to the sod house. She put in a loaf of bread and a jar of jam, a clean white sheet, two white curtains, a strip of new mosquito bar, some towels, a pair of Joan's white stockings, some white bloomers. And last of all, she went to her bureau drawer, and pulled out a flat box. In it lay a new nightgown, embroidered and lace-trimmed, with little knots and roses of palest pink ribbon. It had been Mary Dennison's parting gift, passed through the car window the day she left Platteville.

"When can I use such elegance on the prairie?" Becky had called back through the window.

And Mary, trying to make the parting a little less funereal, had answered gayly, "At your first week-end visit."

And now here was the prairie, the nightgown, and the week-end visit.

Becky hesitated. She wished she had not remembered the gown. Its daintiness would be utterly wasted in that dirty cabin, among the chickens and the flies. That sullen, slovenly woman, who had left a two year old baby exposed to snake bite, certainly deserved no such consideration. Besides, Becky wanted that nightgown herself. From the moment she had seen its sheer folds, its laciness, it had been the apple of her eye. . . That was what Mrs. Kenniker had called Marietta's white dress. . . And yet Marietta would have given up her one and only white gown. . . And Mrs. Kenniker, who had but one Marietta and no money to buy her another gown, would have been willing. . . "In a case of need like this now — "

Becky hesitated no longer. She laid the box on top of the basket and set out on her third trip across the trail. It seemed to her as she entered the open doorway that she had never known what real poverty was until then.

Mrs. Oleson still sat at the table looking into nothingness. Mrs. Kenniker was clearing away the untasted meal.

"No use in coaxing her," she murmured to Becky. "We just got to wait until her crying time comes. Then she'll eat."

Her eyes opened at the sight of the soft white gown. "You ain't intending to cut *that* up!" she whispered.

Becky nodded.

"It's a shame to spoil a lovely thing like that. I'll ride home and get Marietta's dress. That's got the new wore off of it."

"No, you start at this. If you cut it out I can help with the sewing."

Becky turned her face as Mrs. Kenniker's scissors slashed through the gown. "I'll be putting the house in order," she said.

She covered the bed with the sheet, and laid a clean white cloth over the staring red pillows. She put away the food, and stretched a white towel across the table. She washed the window, tacked mosquito bar on the outside, and hung the snowy curtains from the sash before she sat down to her sewing. Mrs. Oleson sat on the stool, not offering to help, and looking at her hands with unseeing eyes. When the gown was finished the two visitors dressed the baby, pulled on the clean white stockings, and smoothed the yellow curls. Then they lifted the little body and laid it on the white bed, covered with the new white mosquito bar, while they put the door back on its hinges and drove out the flies.

One by one the neighbors began to drift in. They brought supplies with them, butter and ham and eggs, baked beans, cake and doughnuts. They brought offers of help, of mourning bonnets, of wagons for the funeral. Three men came with spades to dig the little grave in the soil of the Oleson claim. A neighboring homesteader started out on a ten-mile trip to engage a preacher. Another drove to Winner to send the sad news to the boy down near the Keya Paha River. When, at night-fall, the father drove up the trail with a tow-headed boy on the seat beside him, and a little coffin wrapped in burlap on the wagon floor, there were willing hands waiting to carry in the light burden, to unharness and feed the horses, and to do the evening chores.

Becky helped with the supper before she left. Then she went to take a last look at the dead child. In the only white bed in which she had ever been laid the baby was sleeping, her chubby little hands curled against the lace and the pink ribbons, her yellow curls touching the pink roses. Beside the coffin stood Ole, his long wrists hanging from his flannel shirt, his pale blue eyes looking down at his little sister. He glanced at his mother, sitting humped over on the low stool.

"Come here, Ma," he urged.

Mrs. Oleson did not answer. She twisted her gnarled, brown hands on her knees and kept her eyes on them.

"Come on," he said awkwardly. "You ought to see how sweet she's sleepin'."

The mother slowly left her stool, and looked down at the little girl. Her eyes traveled over the whiteness and daintiness below. Then the tears came, and sobs shook her work-worn frame. "That's the way she should 'a' been kept, always," she said.

BECKY rode back home over the quiet prairie. It was still light, for the days were long in Dakota, but it was the last magical moment of it. Suddenly, like a miracle, the cap of darkness would fall and it would be night. The mourning dove sent out its sad note that always heralded twilight; the little creatures of the grass filled the air with melancholy music. It was as though the prairie itself was sorrowing for the poor Olesons. And the girl again felt that kinship with the country that had been so strong in the spring. It might threaten her, it might turn against her, but the lure was still there. It was the same lure that had brought the Olesons, the Kennikers, the Wubbers. The prairie was her prairie, and the people her people, all held together by the strange bond of needing each other.

THE Linville children, much excited, met her at the end of the trail with a chorus of "Let *me* tell her!"

"We've had visitors," said Dick.

"Mr. and Mrs. Cleaver," yelled Joan and Phil.

"They stayed all afternoon," said Phil.

"They've just gone now," added Joan.

"Too bad I missed them," said Becky, trying to enter into the holiday spirit. "What did they come for? Just a friendly visit?"

"Wanted to know about the school. They've got a teacher for Crane Hollow."

Becky's heart fell. Then Mrs. Kenniker's words had been true. How would they live now! "I know," she said quietly.

"How did you know?"

"Mrs. Kenniker told me when we rode over to Oleson's this morning."

"Then why didn't you tell us at noon, instead of stealing away like the Arabs?"

"I hoped she was mistaken. I still had a faint hope that I might get it; Mr. Cleaver seemed so sure about it when he talked to you."

"What on earth are you talking about? Why, you *are* going to get it!"

"I?" inquired Becky aghast.

"Yes, *you*. Mrs. Kenniker must have been pretty poor at putting the news across! The school commissioner, Mr. Peters, practically promised you the place. You're to drive to Winner to see him Monday, but he says he's only had one other applicant for the job, and that's the oldest Welp boy, the one that lives with his uncle. And Mr. Cleaver said he thought, if you set your mind to it, you might make a better impression than Chris Welp."

Becky got out of the saddle and gave Joan a hug of joy. "I'm too happy for words," she said. "Now let winter come!"

"Mr. Cleaver seemed as tickled as we were," said Dick. "He said that you were the very one for the place. I told him that the Welp kids would probably make trouble for you if you ran against their brother for teacher, and he said if they raised a rumpus in school you were to send them home and make them go to the school board for re-instatement. The board are all home-steaders around here and hate the Welps. That's why the school commissioner was so sure you'd get the job."

Becky went into the house with the children, while Dick put up Job for the night.

"Did you like Mrs. Cleaver?" she asked. "What kind of woman is she?"

"Swell!" said Joan. "She's fat-ish, like him, and curly white hair, and jolly."

"An' not a bit fussy either," put in Phil. "She didn't care a bit how the house looked when she came."

"Oh," said Becky faintly. "How *did* it look?"

"Well, it was kinda mussy," admitted Phil. "You see, the Wubbers came over in the afternoon, and it was so hot in the sun

that we came in here to play. We thought
you wouldn't care. And the Wubbers wanted
molasses on their bread, so we poured some out
of the jug, and too much came out. It kinda got
on the floor. And then we thought we'd play
that Venus was Pete Welp. We wanted Autie
to be him, but he wouldn't, so we had to take
Venus. And we put molasses on her. We didn't
waste it; just took what was already on the floor,
and spread it on her with knives. An' then we
took the big sofa pillow — "

"You said it was too fat anyway," reminded
Joan.

"An' ripped open a corner to let some feathers
out. Only more came out than we expected.
An' then we stuck 'em over Venus."

"What for?" demanded Becky.

"Why, for tar and feathers. We were playing she was Pete Welp being sent out of Tripp
County, like Mr. Wubber said he'd be, some
day."

"Did you undress poor Venus?"

"We didn't have to. She didn't have any too
much on her anyway."

"Did you do all this in the house?"

"We had to. We needed the chairs for the railroad train that we put him on to send him out of the country. That's how the feathers got all over the room."

Becky's heart sank. "Was this before Mrs. Cleaver came?"

"It was just *when* she came. They drove up when we were putting Venus on the train. But she didn't mind the looks at all. She just laughed and laughed. And so did Mr. Cleaver."

Becky groaned. "Where was Dick all this time?"

"Over helping Mr. Wubber fix his harness."

"Oh, we ast 'em to come in," said Joan with pride. "We knew you'd want us to. An' Mr. Cleaver said: 'What you playing, you young villains?' An' they watched us till we were done with the game, an' then Mrs. Cleaver helped us wash Venus, an' told Mr. Cleaver to pick up the feathers. An' he got down on his hands an' knees an' did it. Only some stuck tight. We got a little molasses on the red chair, an' we never knew it till he sat down there. An' then Dick came home, an' invited them to stay for supper. An' they did."

"I'm glad that ham was boiled," said Becky. "What else did you have?"

"We didn't bother cutting the ham. We had fried eggs an' jam an' bread an' milk. Dick fried fourteen eggs, an' we ate 'em all. They said not to make any trouble for them, an' we didn't. Dick served the eggs right from the frying pan so we wouldn't have so many dishes to wash."

Becky gasped. Knowing her family, she felt sure that her picturization of the scene of hospitality was unerring. "Why didn't you get our regular kind of a meal? There was plenty in the house."

"Because she kept telling us not to bother. I didn't want her feeling uncomfortable because we were standing over the stove cooking for her."

"You certainly avoided that. Did she eat anything?"

"She ate three eggs," said Joan, "An' a lot of bread an' butter, an' she asked who made that julicious jam. She said we were to tell you that she didn't know when she'd laughed so much. And she wants us all to come an' see them in Dallas; spend a night with them, she said. They've got room enough for all of us. An' she left a basket of peaches for you and said we couldn't eat 'em till you said so. May we each have one now?"

THEY buried the Oleson baby the next day. There was no room in the crowded sod house to keep the little dead child longer. Dick and Becky rode over the dry trail on horseback. On a corner of the Oleson claim the neighbors had dug an oblong strip of sod out of the withered grass. The hole below looked large for so small a baby. The little white coffin made its last trip in the Oleson farm wagon, with the father driving and the mother and brother sitting on the jolting floor beside it. Ole's eyes were no longer pale blue, but red, and he kept his cap down over them. His long fingers worked nervously. A few neighbors followed in a slow procession. They had not been able to find a minister. Mr. Oleson lifted the coffin from the wagon, and they all followed to the side of the grave. A meadow-lark called its six clear notes, and a gopher sat and watched. It seemed so terrible, thought Becky, to lay that baby away without a prayer, like a dead animal. Would no one say anything? She looked about at the shy, self-conscious faces of her neighbors, and saw that none would. Then she began the Lord's prayer.

The little procession filed back as it had come, leaving a dark mound rising above the flat prairie. Becky, who had feared to leave the children alone on the claim for even so short a time, did not follow, but she and Dick turned their horses toward home. As they neared the prairie dog town they heard a horse coming rapidly down the trail behind them. They both turned to look. It was Ole Oleson, galloping to overtake them. They reined their horses and waited.

Ole had been so full of his errand that he had not considered his shyness, but as his horse stopped the blood rushed to his face and his tongue was tied.

"Did you want us, Ole?" asked Becky gently.

The boy ducked his head awkwardly. "Yes," he said. "I got to tell you — I haf to say — " He could go no further; the tears filled his eyes. "I pay you back sometime," he said. Then he wheeled his horse and galloped away.

CHAPTER IX

SCHOOL

THE NEXT few days Becky spent in reviewing compound interest, trying to persuade her conscience that she was capable of teaching a school, and dreading the approaching meeting with the School Commissioner. But the conference, when it came, was anything but fearful. Mr. Peters was a man of convex profile and easygoing manner, who was frankly relieved at the prospect of getting *any* teacher for the Crane Hollow school.

"There never were people who want teaching

more than homesteaders," said he, "and there's never a place where you'll find fewer teachers than in homesteading country. That school stayed closed all last winter because I couldn't scare up a soul to take it."

"You know I have no teacher's certificate," explained Becky. "I was just ready to enter normal school when we came out here."

"Well, according to state law every teacher has to have a certificate. But a certificate without a teacher isn't of as much good as a teacher without a certificate."

"In other words," said Becky, dimpling, "I'm better than an empty chair. But do you think I can carry a school?"

"If what your school record and Mr. Cleaver says about you is true, you can. He thinks you're about right."

"He knows me as a homesteader, not as a schoolteacher. I suppose I may be better than no teacher at all. The course seems simple enough; the only two things that I'm really afraid of are cube root and the Welps." She explained the feud with her neighbors.

"You won't have to teach cube root. And if the Welp boys make trouble, sit on 'em hard. Their older brother, Chris, who was brought up by an uncle in Bonesteel, wanted the school, and they'll probably not like your getting it. But if they start anything you fire them. I'll stand by you."

Becky repeated this conversation to her family. Joan, especially, seemed impressed. "That's just what I've always thought," she said. "We've been too hold-your-tongue-y to that family; just sat and let them run over us. If they dare to act up in school you do just as Mr. Peters says, an' sit on 'em hard. If you don't, I will!"

"You'd better keep out of trouble, and let Becky fight her own battles," advised Dick.

"Fighting's no trouble to me," observed Joan.

"Maybe I can find a way to get on the good side of them," said the prospective teacher.

" 'There's no good road to a wasp's nest,' Uncle Jim used to say. Don't waste time hoping for anything from the Welps but cussedness."

"It's the arithmetic problems that worry me more than the Welps. When I think of teaching them how to measure a cistern I shake in my boots."

"Keep away from cubic dimensions, and stick to farm problems, where you only have length and width," advised Dick. "Go heavy on reading, grammar, and history, and soft-pedal the rest. *We'll* never give you away! And when you're up against a problem postpone the lesson and let the whole school sing. Many a teacher has done that in my time. I'll bet it's the system that all normal schools teach."

SCHOOL opened on September fifteenth. As Becky crossed the bare fields to the little schoolhouse, nestled in a hollow of the rolling prairie, she saw the homesteaders gathering the remnants of their crop and plowing under the burnt fields, with hope for a better year. Those who had been on the ground the year before worked feverishly, knowing how much must be accomplished before the cold weather set in. Winter was evidently a thing to dread on the Dakota prairies.

The school was an unpainted frame building, with a dejected-looking flight of steps to its only door. Inside was a fat soft-coal burner, some old desks, resurrected from another school, a pine table, two chairs, a blackboard, and a map of the United States. Becky had come early with a purpose in her mind, and a large market basket on her arm. Out of the basket came new sash-curtains to cover the glaring windows, some gay pictures to be tacked on the bare walls, a pot of Wandering Jew for the wide window sill, an American flag to be hung above the blackboard, and a handful of books. Becky and Dick had spent a day cleaning the room the week before, but these little touches made it a cheerful as well as a shining place. The earliest arrivals found a pleasant school and a smiling teacher. Becky was quaking inside, and her dimples had disappeared, but she was trying to remember Uncle Jim. "Hurricanes always whistle before they strike," she could almost hear him say.

One by one they filed in, with books and lunch-boxes — the three little Wubbers; Phil and Joan (Dick had ridden horseback to Winner to enter high school that morning); Marietta, with her shining eyes; the two Courtland boys; four of the Welp children, Pete, Bill, and two freckled-faced girls; the Trainer twins; Johnny Lambert and his sister Shirley; and, towering over the heads of all, Ole Oleson, with his great hands dangling below his coat-sleeves. They were all in the lower grades except the two Lambert children and Marietta, and Becky began to recover confidence as she saw how elementary most of the lessons would be. The two little Welp girls seemed inoffensive children, and the boys, while evidently on the defensive, showed no open rebellion. Becky spent the morning in grading the pupils, there was an hour's recess at noon, and at four o'clock lessons had been assigned and recited, and school was out for the day.

It seemed to Becky that she had never worked so hard as during those golden days of September. She was up at half-past five in the morning to get lunches packed, breakfast ready, and housework done, before she left for school. When she came home there was a hot dinner to cook, lessons for the next day to prepare, and the ironing and mending to do. On Saturdays she washed and helped Dick with the farm work. The children themselves cut the sad-looking corn, and tied it into stacks for fodder. They picked the few pumpkins and the cabbage, dug their scanty hills of late potatoes and the rutabagas, and carried them to the cellar. There were a few parsnips too, and some withered turnips. "All the kinds of vegetables you *don't* like," was Joan's comment on their winter's supply. But Becky gave thanks for the tiny stock that had been saved from destruction. It would help so much to relieve the monotony of canned food.

"Wish we had anything to show in the way of flowers," she said sadly, looking out at the sickly line of poppies and cornflowers, with a shabby Castor and Pollux mounting guard at the head. "No chance of taking a picture of the vines that were torn down, and the plants that burnt up. It wouldn't prove anything to the Land Office except desolation."

"We'll take a kodak of the house, anyway," said Dick. "General Land Office would know we were establishing 'permanent residence' if he saw our awning and our curtains and the little trees. And some day I'm going to get a snapshot of the Welp establishment as I drive by. The two pictures will be Exhibit One and Exhibit Two when the contest comes on."

"That ole contest!" exclaimed Phil gloomily. "I wouldn't mind living without things if I only knew the land was going to be ours. But if I'm going without ice cream sodas and cherries and circuses just to make a farm for Pete Welp I'll be sore that I wasted my life out here."

"I can't think that they'll ever win the contest," said Becky hopefully. "Anyway, there's nothing for us to do except stick it out. And that isn't going to be so hard now. We'll have my salary, if we haven't any crops."

"Good thing we have," said Dick, an old look coming over his merry face. "The fall breaking, the coal for the winter, and the fodder we'll have to buy will take every cent we have. Your salary will have to carry us through the winter, and buy seed for next spring."

"You're not counting the rent."

"Nothing to count on. We didn't have any check at all in August, and none so far this month. I hate to admit it, but for once in her life Aunt Jule was right about those Glovers."

"Well, we can live off the school if we have to," said Becky cheerfully. "And buy seed for next spring, too. Forty-five dollars a month goes a long way."

"If we *have* the claim by that time," remarked Phil.

Dick and Becky made no reply, but each echoed his words in their thoughts.

"I think we ought to start in on the winter's work," went on Becky.

"Plenty of time yet. Summer's hardly over."

"Uncle Jim said that we must start before the cold weather did. Don't you remember how he urged us not to delay?"

"But this is only September."

"Let's get the book and see." She took down the worn, green book, and turned to

SEPTEMBER

Cut corn, dig potatoes, take in vegetables. Get fall breaking done. Have the first breaking re-plowed so snows will sink into ground during

*winter, and have ten new acres to the west plowed
and disked.*

*Don't wait until shivering time to get in your coal.
Buy it from Cleaver, and have it in the cellar by
October 1st. You will need 5½ tons, which you
can haul in two loads.*

*Bank the house to cover entire cellar. On north
side pile it up to the window. Bank stable and
chicken house, and cover tree roots.*

*As soon as you see the first tumble weed get your
hay and straw stacked near the barn, with weights
to keep the wind from carrying them away. See
that your wood is within easy carrying distance
for a ten-below-zero day.*

*Wish I could be around to help you set up stoves,
and then "set around" them with you.*

Dick's eyes, as well as Becky's, were full,
"That means get to work a little harder," he said,
trying to steady his voice. "I'll stop and see
Wubber about the plowing today. And Saturday I'll go in for the first load of coal."

The children were on their way to school in
early October when they saw the first tumble

weed. It came bounding and rolling over the bare prairie like a great ball, until it stopped at their feet. They bent over to look at the queer, spiny leaves that made a globe of brush.

"No wonder they call it 'Russian' thistle," said Joan. "It looks like that bushy Mr. Jarowski, over near the buttes."

Bronx, who always accompanied the children part way to school before he returned to a quiet and uneventful home life, barked loudly. He had run into the deep, dry grass at the edge of the creek, and was pouncing and withdrawing, in a state of wild excitement about something in the grass. The children ran closer, armed with the long sticks they always carried on their prairie walks.

"Probably a snake," said Becky. "Don't go any nearer."

It looked as though a long, dusty-brown hose were gliding through the grass. Bronx followed it at close range. "It's a rattler," said the girl. "Come here, Bronx."

The snake was evidently anxious to get away, but Bronx was so filled with the lure of the chase that he lost all sense of discretion. He rounded the snake, going as near as he dared, and far nearer than was safe.

"Come back here!" commanded Phil.

But Bronx continued to bark wildly, and to follow his prey. The rattlesnake coiled its long, dusty body into a loop, and raised a wicked-looking head.

"Bronx, come back!"

Usually Bronx was an obedient and tractable dog, but he paid no attention to the orders of the children. The end of the snake's tail lifted, and a rattle, as of dry leaves, came from the grass.

"He'll be bitten, like the Oleson baby," quavered Joan.

Becky made a sudden dart at the dog with her lifted stick. Again and again she struck at him savagely. It was not until she had beaten him into submission that he turned tail and left the enemy in the grass.

"You saved him that time," said Phil, as the snake glided away toward the dry creek bed, and Bronx returned, chastened, to the fold.

"It shows how unsafe it is to go empty-handed

on the prairie," said Becky. "Uncle Jim knew what he was doing when he made these snake sticks for us last winter."

"You can't argue with a rattlesnake," he had said as he sat by the open fire, stripping the bark off from these very hickory poles, and fitting a brass ferrule on the end of each. And Becky knew now how right he had been.

THERE was a second battle awaiting Becky at the schoolhouse. The trouble had begun, as the very first trouble in the world began, with an apple. Fresh fruit was next to a miracle in Tripp County, and when the Trainer twins had appeared with a single apple which they were to share at recess, they were the center of an admiring crowd. Pete Welp had seized the fruit from Essie Trainer's hand, and refused to return it. In their struggles to regain their common property the second one of the twins had been thrown down, and her head was bleeding. Marietta, the oldest of the children in the group, had remonstrated with Pete. Becky came up just in time to hear her gentle rebuke and his reply.

Holding the apple safely inside his sweater, Pete bent his back in imitation of Marietta's pathetic curve, and called "What *you* got to say about it, Camel?"

He did not see Becky till she was quite upon him. "Peter, you must give back the apple," she said when she had heard the story.

Pete's reply was to bury his teeth in the fruit, and take a huge bite.

"You must give Essie the apple and apologize to Marietta."

"He'd better give her back the bite," put in Joan.

Pete took another mouthful. There was no time for Becky to consider what was the best discipline. Another bite of that size, and Essie's apple would be beyond recovery.

She stepped to Pete's side, and tried to take the fruit from his hand. The boy resisted. Bill, his younger brother, watched the struggle with delight.

"Don't leave her take it, Pete!" he yelled, jumping up and down with excitement.

Becky was still armed with her snake stick, but

she did not intend to use it except as a final resort. "If you don't give up the apple you may not go in to school," she said, trying to keep her breath and her dignity.

"I'd like to see you keep me out," said Pete. He dodged her out-stretched hand, and took the last of the apple in one huge bite.

Becky hesitated a moment. On her next move hung the success of her winter's school. If she used that hickory stick, that fitted so invitingly in her hand, she might add fuel to the smoldering wrath of the Welps. It might be used against her in the land contest. She thought with fear of the little boys strung up on the hillside, but with righteous indignation, too. If she let this rebellion go by the discipline of her school was lost. Pete towered above her, a broad-shouldered, muscular boy, and she knew that she would be worsted in a physical contest. But if she stopped now she could never command respect or obedience again. She raised the hickory stick.

"Look out, Pete! She's aimin' fer ye," warned his brother.

But the hickory was not needed. Ole, tow-headed Ole, who had just come in to the school yard, set down his dinner pail and approached the group. He was in time to see Pete pull Becky's straw hat off her head, and toss it toward the well.

"You leave your hands off the teacher," warned Ole.

"What's it *to* ye?" demanded Pete.

"I'll show you what," drawled Ole. "Git out of the way thar," he warned the other children.

Pete did not wait for Ole's attack. He struck out and caught the tall Swede on the chin with his fist. The two boys clinched. Becky stepped to one side, uncertain as to what to do. It seemed horrible to let them fight it out like two young animals. Ought she to try to stop it? Then she decided that force was the only language that Pete Welp could understand. "Don't try to talk French to the Fijis," Uncle Jim used to say. Ole was the only one in school who could answer Pete in his own tongue. If Ole should win, Pete would be tamed to submission in school. If Pete won — but Becky turned her thoughts away.

Ole was the taller and more wiry; Pete was

broader-shouldered and more muscular. But he was helpless against Ole's long arms. In two minutes Ole had the school bully down on the ground and was ramming his head into the prairie soil.

"Let him get up now," said Becky.

"You tank you git enough?" queried Ole.

"Yaas," said Pete sullenly.

Ole lifted his long legs from his enemy, and Pete rose slowly to his feet. The blood streamed from a cut on his forehead, and his sweater sleeve was torn loose. He turned on his brother fiercely. "You're a fine guy to leave 'em beat me up!"

Ole pointed sternly to Becky's hat. "You go pick up onct what you threw," he ordered.

Pete brought the hat.

"Now give it to teacher." The boy sullenly obeyed.

"Now, if *she* leaves you stay you kin," said Ole. "But no more of grabbing or such."

"Are you going to behave yourself after this?" asked Becky. "If you are, tell Marietta you are sorry. Then you may come in with the rest of us."

And Pete, with a muttered word to Marietta, came in.

This settled school discipline, as far as the Welps were concerned. Pete was sullen and idle, and he and his brother bullied the younger school children as much as they dared, but they were, on the surface, obedient. And Becky, as she watched their deference toward Ole, was sure that order could be maintained as long as the Swede boy was her pupil. So, though she found the haystack near the barn torn to pieces, and the ax missing from her back door during the week that followed the fight, she accused no one, and did not mention either at school.

Lessons went on smoothly, and Becky began to enjoy, rather than dread, each day's teaching. The walk to and from school over the prairie was a daily pleasure. Becky missed the changing foliage, and the brilliant coloring which made the Platteville autumns so lovely, but the prairie had a fall glory of its own. The faded grass began to show color — patches of orange, and dull red, and rusty brown; the wild ducks flew like an arrow point against the shining clouds; the quail's call sounded through the dry stubble, and a faint haze hung over the world. The dark blue buttes made the only break in the horizon line and showed dimly against the lighter blue sky. The creek began to flow again.

Of all the children in the school Marietta made the best progress. The others welcomed it for the companionship, for the relief from home duties, for the pleasant atmosphere which Becky's merry nature and clever fingers made. But Marietta was a real student, who loved her work as well as her teacher; who never had enough of lessons, and went forward to meet study, instead of dragging it behind her. Her eager eyes glowed over the history and the geography and English, and Becky, for the first time in her life, sensed the inspiration which comes from leading a mind that is so ready to follow. The child hungered for books, and after lending many of her own Becky had an idea that made the Crane Hollow schoolhouse famous for months to come.

"Cold weather is coming on," she said to the school children, one day. "And we all want things to read this winter. If each one of you brought some of your own books to school we could start a little library of our own. Bring whatever you can spare, and we can exchange."

The books came drifting in. Ole brought an old McGuffey's reader and a Farmer's Almanac; the Trainer twins brought "Uncle Tom's Cabin," and "Arabian Nights." Johnny Lambert, whose father was a grocer at Winner, and the only homesteader who seemed to be making a living, donated "Robinson Crusoe," "Hans Brinker," a *Chatterbox,* "Little Men," and "Donald and Dorothy;" the Barnes boys carried in "Dick the Match Boy," "Omoo," and one of the old "Zig-Zag Journeys." Marietta brought in six books, neatly covered with paper, and with her name written in each one: "Vicar of Wakefield," "Neighbor Jackwood," "Tales from Shakespeare," "Byron's Poems," "Life of the Wesleys," and a tattered volume of "Ivanhoe." The Wubber children made a large donation, consisting of "Tempest and Sunshine," "Little Rosebud's

Lovers," "A Cry in the Dark," the "Mystery of the Red Stain," and "The Science of Phrenology." The Welp girls presented a Sears-Roebuck catalogue, and Becky contributed "Eight Cousins," "The Bird's Christmas Carol," "Greek Heroes," "Anderson's Fairy Tales," the "Blue Fairy Book" and two bound volumes of *St. Nicholas.*

Joan looked dubious, as she saw the books taken off the Linville shelves. "That 'Greek Heroes' is mine," she remarked.

"But you don't mind my taking it to school, do you?" inquired Becky. "That's what books are for — to be read."

"That's all right," returned Joan, "But you make those Welp boys understand that they can read with their eyes, and not with their licked thumbs."

Johnny Lambert's father donated a packing case into which the big boys fitted shelves. Then they sandpapered it and coated it with some of the Linville left-over stain. Mr. Cleaver drove out to the schoolhouse one day with the superintendent, and the two men were so impressed by the sight of the well-worn library that Mr. Peters promised her ten dollars from the state fund for more books, and Mr. Cleaver added another five dollars to it. Becky sent for a children's book catalogue, and spent a glorious Sunday afternoon checking off the volumes she could afford to buy. And the fathers and mothers began to read the books that the children carried home.

The weather grew colder. The children who came barefooted to school used to stop on the way, now and then, and squat down to warm their cold feet against their warm bodies. The honk of wild geese became less frequent; the creek had a thin glaze of ice over its surface each morning. The Linvilles set up their base burner, and the red fire glowed a welcome through its isin-glass doors to the children at night. Becky, realizing the discomforts of soft coal, which made a raging fire one moment, and no fire at all the next, appreciated the luxury of the steady warmth, and thanked Uncle Jim, time and again, for the purchase of that dear hard coal stove. She had to rise early to get the lunches packed before she left home, and the school fire started before the pupils arrived; the walk to the schoolhouse grew bleaker as the days went by, the Wandering Jew in the window froze, and the schoolroom was icy in the early morning. But there was fun as well as work during sessions, the days went swiftly by, and when night came there was always the warm house and the cheerful glow of the waiting fire.

The canned goods, ordered and paid for by Uncle Jim last spring, arrived, and were brought out from Dallas by Dick. Mr. Wubber finished the fall breaking, and the barn was stacked with all the fodder it could hold. The awning and the screens were taken down, and the house banked with manure and earth. The Linvilles were ready for winter by the time that snow fell. It came at first with a few light flakes that starred the frozen ground; then a less doubtful dust; then a business-like downfall that went on all night. The prairie dogs took to their holes, the rabbits disappeared from the corn stubble, and on starlit nights the coyotes howled from the hill where the water-mark stood.

Day by day the three children walked the four

miles of the round trip from home to school. After snow fell Dick was warned to stay over night in Winner if there was any prospect of a storm; Becky had heard enough of Dakota blizzards to be fearful of them. But the weather was mild enough except for the biting wind. The children soon learned that frosted ears and noses came from wind, rather than cold, and protected their faces from the worst of the blasts. And Becky rejoiced, in spite of the hardships, that the family was well, and that the Crane Hollow school was hers.

The Welp boys, though openly tractable, were capable of all the small meannesses in which they were not afraid of exposure. At the noon period the children gathered around the school stove to eat their lunches, while they warmed their hot drinks on the flat surface near the pipe. On one of the winter days, Becky, returning from the cellar, saw Pete Welp lean forward from the front of the stove, and take a sandwich off the desk that Autie Wubber had vacated for a moment. He opened the bread and quickly peppered the filling, giving a furtive glance at the two nearest boys. Then he laid it back on Autie's desk, with an innocent expression. Becky was just about to pounce upon him when she caught Johnny Lambert's dancing eyes over Pete's shoulder. Johnny laid his finger on his lip, and Becky held her tongue, waiting to see what the boy would do. Johnny walked over to the wash basin which stood on a shelf behind Pete's back, and took therefrom a cake of soap. Whistling innocently, he passed the rear of the stove where Pete's pail of coffee was heating, and dropped his burden into it as he went by.

Presently Pete went for his coffee. "Trade you sandwiches," said Johnny to Autie, in a low voice. Autie, flattered at being noticed by a fourteen year old, gladly passed over the thick sandwich that lay on his desk, to receive one from Johnny's pail.

Pete watched and waited, but nothing happened. He saw Autie eat his sandwich with unusual relish. Then he lifted his pail to drink the sweetened, creamy, foamy draught that was always the favorite part of his lunch . . .

It was months before the school children stopped the motion of handwashing every time that Pete approached.

It took one more lesson to put the Welp boys in their proper place. And that lesson was not given by Ole or Johnny, but by one of the thin-legged, freckled-faced primary children that the Welp boys designated as "the babies." On the hillside back of the schoolhouse the children gathered to slide during the noon recess. Little Kate Welp had pulled her shabby sled to school one day for the sake of a few rides, and her brother Bill had promptly taken it away from her.

"You give that sled back to your little sister!" called Joan from the bottom of the slope.

"What *you* got to say about it, Skinny?"

"You give it back or you'll find out."

"Like to see *you* make me — or anyone else," said Bill. He threw himself on the sled, lying flat on his stomach, and went down the incline, turning the sled as he went so it would run into the group of small children at the bottom of the hill. But Joan was not in the group when he arrived. She had run up behind him, and before he had had time to rise, had mounted his long frame from the rear. She sat down astride of him with no gentle motion; no ladylike grace. Once, twice, thrice, she raised herself in the air, and came down on the delicate region above the stomach with jounces that threatened to remove all the breath within him.

"That's what you get, Bill Welp," said his torturer. "Mr. Peters *said* we could come down hard on you if you acted up."

Nothing was said about the occurrence in the schoolroom. Becky noticed that Bill had come in from his sleighing somewhat chastened in manner and green about the lips. She intercepted several baleful glances that afternoon between him and Joan, but on the theory that it was well to let sleeping dogs lie, asked no questions. Two days later in Joan's class she assigned, as a language lesson, an essay on "A Bad Boy." And it was from her little sister's paper that she learned Joan's version of the story:

THE BAD BOY

Once ther was a bad boy. They called him "bad boy," he was the wurst boy in scool. His name was Bill. He had no freinds. Once he took his sister's sled and she sade plece give me my sled, and he sade I'd like to see you make me.

He slode down hill on it, and ran into some grils. One of the grils ran up to him and sat on top of him. She bonced three or fore times and verry hard on his stumake. After that he was not so gay. They all sade to the litel gril good for you.

CHAPTER X

SNOW BOUND

A WIND that had started at Labrador was
tearing over South Dakota, howling down
chimneys and sucking through cracks. And
there were plenty of cracks in Tripp County. A
dark sky fell like a cup over the prairies, and the
coyote who lived on the water-mark hill had
stopped howling, and taken himself to winter
quarters.

Inside the Linville house it was snug and warm,
with the base burner glowing, the student lamp

shining, and the kettle near the stovepipe steam-
ing away. The younger fry were abed, and Dick
and Becky were at the table, the boy at his lessons, and the girl correcting papers. Bronx
blinked contentedly behind the stove, the most
luxurious dog in homesteading country. Becky
looked up from her papers presently to see Dick
frowning over a column of figures.

"What's the matter? Stuck on your algebra?"

"It isn't lessons; it's finance. I was figuring
to see if we were going to get through the winter."

"But we had that all decided. We figured
out last month that we were going to get along all
right if nobody was sick. Don't you remember
we had a margin of forty dollars?"

"I know we did, but we were counting the rent
in, then. And I'm afraid we're not going to get
it. They've just paid up for September now.
At any rate, we can't count on it regularly."

"No, I suppose we can't. Mr. Dennison
seemed to think it was better to let them stay on,
rather than try to get new tenants this winter, but
I don't know if we were wise. They may be the
worthless kind who'll *never* pay up. And we'll

need every cent of it when it comes time to buy seed, and make our spring payment on the land."

Dick went on with his figuring. "The money seems to melt away. The coal cost eight dollars more than we counted on; I had to put tar paper against the house before we banked it; and we had to replace the ax. The oil can blew over, and we lost more than ten gallons. Then there were the kids' shoes and our galoshes. If expenses go on in this way we won't have enough left of that forty-dollar margin to cast a shadow. I don't know what we'd do if you didn't have the school."

"Well, we won't go hungry. And, thank goodness, we don't need many clothes out here."

"Except shoes."

"And overalls. Phil's like the woman Uncle Jim used to tell about, who bragged of her son's clothes — 'Just pants and pants and pants.' "

Dick grinned at the family joke, but his face dropped back into worried lines. "Well, I know that we can't spend a cent that we don't have to spend."

"Christmas is coming too," said Becky.

"Swell chance we'll get of a celebration. If we get a good Christmas dinner I'll be satisfied."

"The kids won't. They've been counting on it for weeks. Look at Joan's list. I found it in her spelling book last Monday."

Dear Santa Close
  Plece dont forget to Give Bronx a presat
What I want for Crismase :
  haingkerches
  doll
  books
  games
  a pensl
  candy
  a dolls tronk
  rist wach
  past
  a litel pelo for the doll

"What's a pelo?" inquired Dick.

"Something you sleep on, of course. I can provide that, easily enough, and the 'pensl' and perhaps the paste, but I'm afraid she can't count on a trunk, much less the watch."

"They'll have to do what I'm doing — count without getting any answer. Six months into $300 doesn't leave much when you subtract for seed and payment on land and insurance and food."

Becky bent her eyes on her brother as he went back to his figures. Dick had certainly changed in the last seven months. When he left Wisconsin he had been a careless, happy-go-lucky boy, whose interests were football and skating and the running high jump; who never had a cent in his pocket, nor a worry in his head. And now he was spending the evening over family accounts! He had altered physically, too. His freckles and his rebellious reddish hair were unchanged, but his shoulders had broadened, his merry brown eyes were soberer and steadier, and his mouth was resolute. Tripp County had made Dick a man.

"Well, we're going to have a Christmas," said the girl — "such as it is. I have two blouses for Phil, and two aprons for Joan cut out, for a start, and I've already sent Mary Dennison some money for a game and a book apiece. I'll make some candy and some popcorn balls, and perhaps we can buy a few oranges. That would be a real treat for them. As for you, Dicky, you'll have to take my blessing and a new pair of suspenders."

"Cut out the suspenders, and apply the money on the garden seeds next spring. I planned to subscribe to a couple of magazines for you, but you won't even get the funny page of the *Omaha Bee* now."

"Funny how little you care for the unnecessaries out here. In fact, I never knew what the necessaries *were* until I tried homesteading."

"Food, clothing, and shelter," quoted Dick. "And easy on the clothing, too. All you need is enough to keep heat off in summer and cold off in winter. If I went in to town wrapped in meal-sacks I don't think anybody would look at me twice."

"Four dollars of this month's salary has to go to the school children," went on Becky. "I've sent for a box of crayons and some candy for each one. I'd have a tree for them if there were evergreens within reach of us. I don't think one of them, except the Lamberts, ever had a Christmas.

You ought to hear the questions they ask about it. Venus asked me yesterday if Santa Claus would come if you wrote to Sears-Roebuck about it. I don't suppose the Wubbers ever had a Christmas gift in their lives."

"It'll be a new thing for Phil and Joan to come down to small pickings. Uncle Jim used to have such a whale of a Christmas for us all."

Both children were silent. They could see Uncle Jim standing on the step-ladder, fastening the gold star on the treetop; Uncle Jim sawing away down cellar at the toy boats and doll houses he always produced at Christmas time; Uncle Jim coming in on Christmas eve, with bulging pockets, shining eyes, and flecks of snow powdering his coat. . . The old Christmases never could come back to Becky and Dick. They would do their best for the younger children, but it was Uncle Jim that had made the holiday for them.

THE last week of school before vacation was bitterly cold, and it took real heroism to make the two daily trips. The whole prairie was changed by the snow; the black line of the creek-bed was the only landmark left. The sky seemed to drop lower over the gray waste, the cold bit into fingers, and the snow drove into cheeks like needles. The two little Welps came to school with their hands wrapped in cloth, and though Becky longed to give them mittens when she saw their poor, frost-bitten fingers, she dared not venture. She was glad, for their sakes, when the Christmas program was over, and the school dismissed for the holidays.

Three days before Christmas Becky heard a timid knock on her back door, and opened it to find Crystal Wubber, breathless, and with a big bundle in each hand. "Miss Linville, kin I leave these things at your house until Christmas?" she inquired. "I been getting some giffs fer the kids and they mistrust something's going on. I know they'll find 'em if I keep 'em at home."

Her worried little face looked relieved, as Becky promised their safe-keeping. "They ain't no spot to hide things over to our house," she said, "Except under the bed, and that's ma's place. An' Miss Linville, I want to ask you something else." She unwrapped an unwieldy bundle, covered with newspapers. Out of it fell a giant tumble weed, its spiny leaves dried on its skeleton stalk; its bushy top mounted on a trunk made of a broomstick. "Do you think that would do fer a Christmas tree?" she asked.

Becky looked at the dry bush with softened eyes.

"I thought maybe I could use some plum brush fer a tree," went on the child. "But I just hate the switchey look of 'em for Christmas. So when this whopper tumble weed came along last fall it stuck in our chicken wire, and I hung it up in the barn. It dried just that way, and I thought maybe the childern would like it fer a tree. The little ones never seen no pictures of one, even, and they wouldn't know if it wasn't just like. I got a pail of sand to stick that broomstick down in. I could hang the popcorn and the light things on the tumble weed, and put the rest around it. Do you think that would work, Miss Linville?"

"I'm sure the children would love it."

Crystal opened the second bundle. There were

strings of popcorn, and chains of colored paper; there was a corncob doll for Venus, a wagon made out of a codfish box for Autie, a ball wound of rags for Twinkle; and there were three sticks of candy.

"This is fer ma," said Crystal. It was the shallow lid of an oatmeal carton, covered with a scrap of black velvet and a ruffle of tarnished gold lace. "Mis' Lambert give me those pieces. I been savin' 'em a long time. It's fer ma to put her thimble on, an' thread. She ain't got no thimble — she allus uses the arm of the chair to push — an' she don't sew very much anyway. But it's nice to have in a room. An' I'm going to give pa this stamp. I found it in the store, an' when I turned it in to Mister Lambert he said I might keep it. Pa ain't got no folks but us, and he can't but just write his name, but if he *had* to write a letter, ever, there'd be the stamp!"

As Becky commended and admired a plan grew. She could hardly wait until the little girl had gone to tell the rest of the Linvilles about it. Dick and Phil and Joan looked over the pitiful little hoard of 'giffs,' and became, by compari-

son, not poor homesteaders, but Lords and Lady
Bountiful. The Wubbers could certainly,
surely, have a Christmas.

"I'll make one of those boats that you work
with a rubber band," said Dick.

"I'll give them my flinch game," said Phil.

"They can have my jacks," offered Joan.
"And I'll put in the glass prism with a thermometer on it for Crystal. You can always be looking at a thermometer in Dakota — either it's too
far up or too far down. And she didn't have
one thing saved for herself."

During the three long winter evenings that followed the Linville children were busy under
the student lamp. Under Becky's deft fingers
a whole family of paper dolls sprang and were
costumed; a jumping Jack and a Jack-in-the-box,
as well as the boat, were evolved by Dick, and
the two younger children traced outline pictures
for the Wubber crayons. Becky added a thimble
that she felt was large enough to fit Mrs. Wubber's finger, and some popcorn balls and candy
from their own store. And on the afternoon before Christmas, when the north wind blew Crys-

tal across the snowy prairie to collect her gifts,
she carried away in the big bundles a number of
treasures that would be a surprise the next day
to the little girl herself.

"I'll store 'em in the barn till morning," said
Crystal joyously.

"Does your mother know about them?"

"No, ma'm," responded Crystal, "I ast her
about it in the first place an' she said Christmas
was just one thing too many fer her. So it'll be
a supprise on her, too. Thanks, Miss Linville,
and Merry Christmas. Ain't that what folks
say?"

"Merry Christmas to you, dear," said Becky,
as she let the little girl out of the door with an
affectionate hand on her shoulder. She stood
at the window looking at the small figure until
it disappeared around a bend in the trail. It
was gray and desolate on the prairie. On either
side of the road stretched the miles of snow, un-
broken except by the shabby cornstalks that made
the lonely landscape look still more forlorn.
Over the snowy wastes bent the metallic gray
sky.

Becky's thoughts went back to Platteville as it had been a year ago. The little church, hung with greens and lighted with candles; the jolly crowds in the street; the carols of the children at every door. And Uncle Jim, carrying home the Christmas turkey himself, "so the delivery boy won't be tempted to abscond," buying new scarlet decorations for the tree — "Red's a poor color for a patch, but a good color for candles, Beck;" unpacking Phil's new fire engine — "Now, how do you think *that* will suit our fire chief!" All the dear old memories that hung around the holidays came rushing back: the unimportant little speeches and doings that a mind treasures so long after the real things are dust and ashes.

Out on the prairie there was no reminder of the day. Not a candle in a window, not a wreath at a door, not even a Christmas card in the store at Winner. She had done her best to right things for the children, to help the Wubber family to a Christmas, to bring some little observance of the day into the lives of her pupils. But for herself she knew that there *could* be no Christmas with-

THEY MOVED SLOWLY ALONG IN THE BITING
SWEEP OF THE STORM

out Uncle Jim. . . She turned away from the window and went back to her work. The three children were out in the barn hunting for eggs that had become so scarce since cold weather set in, and the house was so still that the kettle's hum was noisy. She glanced at the dressed chicken that they had sacrificed for tomorrow, at the covered dish that held the popcorn balls, at the little pile of gifts that she had made ready for the children. And then she put her head down on the kitchen table, and cried — not noisy weeping, but dry, broken sobs for the year that had gone and taken Uncle Jim.

THERE was the sound of wheels outside. Bronx barked joyously, and the children shouted with delight. Becky had just time to dry her eyes and push back her hair. There was a great stamping of snow on the back steps, and in came Mr. Cleaver, with Phil and Joan holding a hand apiece, and Dick behind him.

"Santa Claus has come!" cried Joan. Red-faced and fur-coated, the guest didn't look un-like that Christmas visitor.

"I've come to get, instead of to give," he announced. "Mrs. Cleaver has sent me to bring you in to her for Christmas."

The children shrieked for joy. "Tomorrow?" asked Becky.

"Today. Right now. Up to yesterday we expected to go to Omaha for Christmas. But that's fallen through, and we don't intend to have the whole day spoiled. When my wife suggested that we have the fun of four kids in the house I couldn't wait to get started out this way. You're to come back with me, spend the night and tomorrow, and I'll bring you back late Christmas afternoon."

"All of us?"

"The whole bunch, including Bronx. We want to see how it will go to have some kid stockings hanging beside ours. Hustle up and get your duds on. Wrap up, too; that's a real Christmas wind coming from the north."

It was queer how that desolate sweep of snow-fields lost its lonely look as the big car sped along the trail. The menace disappeared from the sky that hung so low, and there was a hint of holiday in the wind that had seemed so threatening. Mrs. Cleaver met them at the door of the Dallas home; a soft, motherly woman with red cheeks, who had a cup of hot soup for each one, and a roaring fire in the furnace. They had an early supper, and while the other children went to a Christmas entertainment with Mr. Cleaver, Mrs. Cleaver took Becky off down Main Street with her.

"We didn't dare plan anything until we were sure we could have you," she said. "Now we've got to work fast."

In the little frontier town she found a jointed doll for Joan, a wonderful box of paints for Phil; and a sweater for Dick: candy and nuts and oranges, and even a tiny Christmas tree.

"Oh, Mrs. Cleaver, you mustn't!" protested Becky, shocked at the size of the doll, and the splendor of the sweater.

"Becky Linville," said her hostess. "I haven't put a doll in a stocking for ten years. *Don't* spoil things!"

After the younger ones were abed, Dick and Becky helped trim the tree and filled the stock-

ings with the Christmas things they had brought
from home at Mr. Cleaver's suggestion.   Becky
caught the quick look that passed between Mr.
and Mrs. Cleaver as the little bundle of home-
made gifts was opened, but she didn't mind it
for some reason.   It seemed sweet to be pitied, to
be petted, to be treated like a little girl, instead
of the head of a family.   It was lovely, too, to
be kissed good-night; to be told that you were
"plucky kids to have stuck it out;" and that it was
far nicer for the Cleavers to *have* you there than
for you to be there.   As she crept into bed beside
Joan, Dakota didn't seem so different from Platteville, after all.

It took a moment for Becky to remember where
she was when she woke in the gray Christmas
morning in the rosy room, a real room, with
hangings and pictures, and a pink shaded light.
Joan opened her eyes sleepily.   "Is it six?" she
asked.   "Mrs. Cleaver said we might get up at
six."

"You mustn't get up till we know that they're
awake."

But the Cleaver family were astir first, and by

the time the guests were dressed the tree was lighted, and a fire was burning in the fireplace downstairs. And in Becky's stocking, which had not been hung the night before, there was a slender silver necklace that made her eyes fill.

It was a happy, homey day, with a wonderful Christmas dinner, and a quiet afternoon spent around the fire. Little by little most of the story of the lonely year came out, and the children felt cheered and warmed and heartened. The sympathy and interest did as much as the homelike surroundings to make the day perfect. When at four o'clock they kissed Mrs. Cleaver good-by and got into the car to drive back across the prairie, they felt that they were parting with an old friend.

"This is just the beginning," said Mrs. Cleaver. "We're going to have you often, after this."

And Mr. Cleaver, as he left them at the door of their house, said almost the same thing. "People without kids, and kids without people ought to get together," he added as he drove away.

CHRISTMAS was one of the two events of that year. The other happened in February when the children had begun to feel that the backbone of the long winter was broken. There had been a thaw, and a period of golden sunshine and mild weather that almost hinted of spring. Then came a day when the gray clouds hung low, and a biting wind sprang up. Before Dick rode off on horseback to high school Becky warned him that if it looked like snow he was to stay in Winner all night. She and the children packed their lunch, and went off to school together. Ole Oleson had just gone along that trail, but the wind had already swept away his tracks, and was making wave-marks on the snow that was left in the ravines. All day long Becky kept glancing uneasily out of the window, for the clouds looked threatening, but it was not until after two that the snow began to fall. It came at first with a few doubtful flakes that the wind quickly whirled away. After that followed a downfall so thick that in ten minutes she could not see to the coal shed. It was driven obliquely by a gale that came from the northeast.

"I think we'll dismiss school," she said. "It's nearly time to go home, anyway, and it looks as though a storm were on the way." They skipped the final school song, and put on their coats at once. Becky turned off the drafts of the stove, and they all started out of the building together.

As she closed the door the wind caught her, and slammed her back against the schoolhouse. The blizzard was not coming; it was here. She took the hands of the smallest children, but she was soon forced to leave them and herd them into single file. The older children started on first, and Becky followed in their trail, breaking the path for the little ones behind her. They wavered in the wind, and moved slowly along, their heads bent to avoid the biting sweep of the storm. Several times the teacher had to stop and wait for her followers. When she looked up after one of these waits the older group were not to be seen; the driving snow hid them from sight. With her were the three little Wubbers, the two Welp girls, Phil and Joan, Shirley Lambert, and the Trainer twins, the babies of her flock. She knew that with their slow progress she could not catch up with the others.

The sky was a gray cover, dropped low over the earth. The drifting flakes flew like wild things. The snow that had covered their feet now covered their ankles; soon reached nearly to their knees. The children stopped complaining and stumbled slowly along, while Becky encouraged them with all the breath she had left. The first houses on the trail were only a mile and a half from the schoolhouse; they must reach one of them before the storm grew worse. But the storm did not wait. It swept round them in a dizzying whirl that bit and stung wherever it touched. The new snow had fallen on a soft layer below that made walking very difficult. The Trainer twins complained that their feet were heavy, and that they were too tired to go on, but Becky insisted on it, cheering, encouraging, and even lifting them over the gullies where the snow was deepest. It was not until she saw how swiftly it was growing dark that she realized that the outlook was serious for the children. The older ones were probably safe by that time; they must have reached one of the two claim houses that were directly opposite each other on the trail. But at the rate they were going now the others could never reach there. Alone, she could make the shelter, but the children never could. She tried to estimate how far they had come, and finally decided that it was a shorter distance back to the school than it was on to the Emerson home. So she turned her little band. They would be safe in the schoolhouse until they were called for.

How Becky ever got them back to the building she never knew. It meant an hour of determined effort, of patient plodding; of constant urging and commanding, and even scolding. She finally herded them in a line that moved slowly forward, each holding on to the one ahead. The wind battered their faces; the snow blinded them; the smallest ones cried and begged for a rest. Many, many times the line was forced to stop while she went to the rear to cheer, to admonish, to pick up the fallen. The snow was so heavy that she did not see how the short legs could lift themselves out of the drifts. But somehow they succeeded. The prairie was a storm-tossed sea, and out of its depths the little band of castaways struggled and floundered to the schoolhouse door. Becky herded them, crying and wringing their half-frozen fingers, back into the school. Hobbling about on her stiff feet, she opened the draughts of the stove, and out of blue lips spoke cheerily:

"Here is the best place for you until your people come for you. The storm can't get at us here." But as she spoke she gave an uneasy glance through the window at the whirling snow. Unless they arrived in a few minutes there would be no coming, that night.

As the room grew warm the children began to thaw out. Becky left them to their games while she began to take stock. She would have to prepare for a siege, for if the snow went on they would have to stay in the schoolhouse all night. That meant fuel, and the soft coal was piled in the shed, back of the school. It meant trip after trip through that blizzard to get enough to last all night, for the week's supply had grown low. It didn't seem a possible thing to walk through

that driving snow, and carry a basket of coal besides, but it must be done, and done soon, too,
for it was already dark out-of-doors. It might
even be that she could not find her way now
through that storm.

In the box of shelves that served her for a
school cupboard lay a ball of light rope that
Becky had used for the curtain at the Christmas
program. It was not long enough to reach to
the coal shed, but it would help. To it she added
Joan's sled rope and a long doubled length of
heavy twine. She put on her outer garments
again, and opened the door. The wind almost
tore it from her grasp, and she stepped out into
a drift of snow at the steps. She rounded the
schoolhouse, feeling her way in the dark along
the siding, and tied the end of her rope on to the
heavy shutter on the back window. With the
other end in her hand she started out through the
driving snow in the direction of the shed. It took
her five minutes to reach the little building fifty
feet away. She tied the rope to the hasp on the
door, and filled her basket from the pile of soft
coal. Going back was somewhat easier, for the

wind was at her shoulders, and she had the rope for a guide. But even at best it took every effort that she could muster, and she arrived at the school door almost exhausted.

"You shan't go out again," said Joan. "I'd sooner freeze."

"Leave me go, too," begged Crystal. "I kin help."

The other children joined in Joan's plea, but Becky knew the demands that night would make on the fire, and with only a moment's rest she went out into the storm again. After the second trip she dared not wait even that long, for she knew that a moment's delay would cover her track.

Back and forth she struggled between shed and school. Blinded, weary, stiff with cold, she made her way through the drifts, realizing now why people froze from exposure. It was so much easier to lie down and die than to make the effort to go on. Nine trips she made with her heavy basket. On the tenth the rope came apart, her burden dropped, and it was with the greatest exertion that she made her way back to the school.

She found her charges restless and worried. Even they had begun to see that rescue that night was impossible.

"Phil was just putting on his galoshes to go out after you," said Venus. "We thought you were lost."

It was half-past five, and pitch dark in the schoolhouse. Becky thawed out her half-frozen hands and feet, and lighted the gasoline lamp. There would be enough gasoline to last a couple of hours. Then she asked about lunch pails. Some had been dropped in the storm; others were empty. Among them all were two sandwiches, a doughnut, a piece of corn-bread and a large piece of cheese. Becky divided these among the children, heated water on the stove, and made each one drink a cup of it. Then she set them to playing games again; the more they exercised the longer she could make the fuel last. She doled out her coal sparingly, but it seemed to melt away in the draught made by that wind. It was the night that the young teacher dreaded, after they grew too tired to play. How could she keep them warm against that wind, that rat-

tled the windows and made the flimsy little building tremble? White frost filled every crack.
The children shivered if they left the circle
around the fire.

Before eight the snow had mounted above the
window-sills, and the lamp burned low. The
youngest children began to get sleepy. Becky
covered the floor around the stove with every bit
of paper she could find in the schoolhouse. She
spread out old newspapers, tablet sheets, open
school books, the big map — everything she could
find that she could use to keep the wind out. On
them she grouped the children, each one in his
outer garments, even to mittens. Over them she
spread the big piece of ticking that Mr. Lambert
had loaned them for a curtain at their Christmas
entertainment. That was all she could do except to keep up the fire. All night she fed the
stove while the wind raged and howled outside.
Sometimes she drowsed for a moment in her
chair; sometimes she walked to keep awake. But
the children slept, and though she was sure that
they were stiff and chilly, she knew that they
would not freeze so long as she was there and
the coal lasted.

It was hours later when Venus Wubber set up a cry of discomfort that woke the others. Becky held up a match to the school clock and saw it pointed to six. For a moment she thought it had stopped the night before; then she realized that the windows were covered with snow, and that while it was dark in the room, it must be day outside.

The pile of coal that she had dumped into the room the night before was nothing but a heap of dust with three small pieces atop. There would be no fire to depend on now.

The room was already growing cold. She had some trouble in persuading the children, who thought it was still night, that exercise was necessary. But she finally got the stiff feet in use, and the lame arms in motion. She knew that exercise must be kept up, perhaps all day, if the children were to be spared. They marched, they sang, they played games in that dark room for hours, and it seemed to Becky that each hour was a day.

"I'll never want to play pom, pull away, again as long as I live," said Joan, and the other children echoed it. They were hungry and tired and

cold and irritable.   They were frightened, too,
when they caught a glimpse of the snow wall that
blocked the doorway.

"Will we ever get out again?" quavered Essie.

"I'll get you out if you'll all do what I tell
you," said Becky.   She only half believed it, herself, but she must not let them know that.   She
encouraged, and petted, and pleaded; she de-
vised games; she took part in all the calisthenics;
she made marching in a dark room a funny play.
The children clumped around after her on half-
frozen feet, they cried over their aching hands,
and they pleaded to be allowed to rest.   But the
girl was firm.   By nine the wind had begun to
die down.   At eleven a little crack of light shone
through the upper part of the sash, and they
could see the reflection of a brilliant sun.   And
at two in the afternoon, when Becky was leading
her weary flock through a "hopping march,"
there was the sound of shovels outside — of shovels and voices and safety.

It was Dick's voice that she heard first, and
Dick's anxious face peered through the schoolroom door when the drifts of snow had been

plowed away. What he said was "Gee!" but there was relief and joy enough in that one word for Becky to remember all her days. After him came Mr. Peters and a procession of the neighborhood men, who pounced in turn upon the children.

Mr. Peters looked around at the cold stove, the cold room and the blue-faced children. "How did you keep them from freezing?" he asked.

"She marched us," said one of the Trainer twins. "She's kep' us going it all day. We're all in!"

"How about *you?*" inquired Mr. Peters, with a keen look at the heavy-eyed teacher.

But Becky was not too tired to smile. "All in, but *all out!*" she said.

CHAPTER XI

THE CALL OF THE PRAIRIE

THE SNOW melted as rapidly as it fell.
Five days later the roads were clear, and
a delegation of homesteaders drove into Winner, and visited the commissioner of schools.
Mr. Cleaver, dropping in for a call at the same
place, met a delegation of them filing out.

"Who are your friends?" he asked, helping
himself to a chair in Mr. Peters' office.

"Committee from Crane Hollow. Come in
to talk about your protégé who's teaching out

there. Seems there's one homesteader out that way that's making trouble about her. Man named Welp."

"I know him," said Mr. Cleaver grimly.

"Well, he's got a son who wants that school. The Welp family are low down, good-for-nothing trash, but the boy's different from the rest; was brought up by an uncle who gave him quite a bit of schooling. Young Welp applied for the school last summer, but I gave it to Miss Linville, on the ground that she'd had more education. Now the uncle is giving him a year of normal training which little Miss Linville never had, more's the pity. And old Welp is talking big about this being her last term; that next year his boy will get the school."

"Anything *to* the talk? You're the one to decide that, I should say."

"Well, it's a mean sort of thing to decide. We're doing our best to raise the standard of teachers out here, and I've talked education for them till I'm blue in the face. Technically, the young man's had the better preparation."

"Do the people out that way want him?"

"Want him! They want Miss Linville, and no one else. That's what that delegation came in to tell me. They were solid for her before the blizzard — said she'd done wonders for the whole community, as well as the children — but now they're determined to keep her. I don't wonder they are; there wouldn't be any children left to *make* a school if it hadn't been for her. They would have been frozen stiff, just like that man they found two miles away from the school-house the day after the storm."

"You haven't any idea of letting her go, have you? You'd be an idiot if you did."

"No, I shan't let her go, even if I have to eat my words about raising teaching standards. She may not have had the preparation, but she's a fine girl, and a born teacher. We're lucky to have her. No, I wouldn't think of giving the place to Welp."

"Then I suppose the delegation went away satisfied."

"Well, partly. If Welp wins the contest on that land the young Linvilles will have to leave Tripp County. The delegation came partly to see if I couldn't induce him to give up the contest."

"Just how did they think you were going to bring that about?"

"Oh, they weren't particular about the method. Persuasion or poison — anything, just so they could keep her. They're dead set on that."

"I don't blame them. She's a fine little woman. But I don't know how you, or anyone else, for that matter, are going to get a wedge under Welp. He's an ornery customer."

"That's what I told them. They were mighty disappointed; seemed to think I could put the man out of the country if I only wanted to. It was an amusing kind of interview, in spite of the earnestness of the committee. That fat, dark woman that headed the procession did most of the talking."

"Name's Wubber, isn't it?"

"Yes, she's a neighbor of Miss Linville's, and strong for her. Says she has more ee-nergy than any one she ever saw. 'That's what I admire,' she told me. 'I got a lot of it in me, and I always like to see it in others. Mighty few girls of her age has got her git up and git.' "

"She's right about that," said Mr. Cleaver heartily.

"You're sold to her, too, are you?"

"I am that. And I'm not the only one in my family that is. She spent Christmas day with us, and my wife fell for her, hard. I don't know when I've seen her taken with anyone as she was by that slip of a girl. When she read the story of Becky's siege during the blizzard she said it didn't surprise her, she knew that the girl would stand up under anything. She's a plucky kid; just see how she's carried on during this hard year, keeping that family fed and mothered, besides running the school! She never was used to hard living before, either; it must have been tough work for her out here in the beginning."

"Yes, she's got a lot of grit. You can see that by her work in school. Country teaching is a good test of a young person, with the long walks, the building of fires and the carrying of water, besides the lessons. Miss Linville has done every bit of that herself, rather than hire one of the big boys to do it, as most of my teachers do. Oh, she's done a lot for that community — parents as well as children. You may be sure I'll not let her go as long as I can keep her."

"I wish that Welp would let her alone. Don't believe he'll ever succeed in getting the claim away from them, but he can keep them stirred up, just as he's done ever since they arrived."

"Maybe the neighbors will be able to do something with him. They left saying that if no one else could get him out they were going to take matters into their own hands."

"What did they mean?"

"I didn't inquire. Better not be too inquisitive in a country where the sheriff lives miles away from trouble."

"You're right about that," said Mr. Cleaver.

THE same delegation that had waited upon Mr. Peters visited the Crane Hollow school a few days later. It had been a hard day for Becky, for the children had been unusually trying and stupid, and in the absence of Ole, who was out of school for the day, the two Welp boys had been impertinent and disorderly. At the noon period, while the children were out playing with what was left of the snow, Becky was bent over spelling papers. She was smiling as she corrected Joan's, who had found time, while waiting for the others to finish, to add to her sheet a few patriotic thoughts:

My Contry is avey swee land of libery of tey I sing
Oh say can you see by the danser lee light
Oh buetiful for spay shuss skies for am burst wave of grane

"One hundred per cent on the lesson that she commits to memory," thought Becky. "About six per cent on the extemporaneous spelling. Which side of her paper is the real test?"

There was a bang on the window, and a snowball crashed through the glass, and struck the hot stove, hissing as it melted. Becky looked out of the window, but there was no sign of the culprit. She covered the broken pane with a piece of pasted paper, and went on with her work. When the pupils filed in in response to the school bell, she questioned them about the broken glass.

All denied it, Peter Welp the most vociferously of all.

"It was you that threw it, Pete Welp," accused Shirley Lambert.

"It was not, you little liar!"

"It was him, Miss Linville," put in one of the Trainer twins. "He was aiming at me when he did it." And there were several other voices that rose in the accusation.

Becky was pleasant, but firm. "Peter, the school commissioner won't mend our windows for us. Ask your father to send us a pane of glass, and you and William can set it for us."

"You see me doing that, don't you?" inquired Pete, for the benefit of the school. "You can't prove that I broke that window. If you say I did you're a liar. Whoever says I did it is a liar, and he's got to fight me."

"It will be an all-school fight, then," said Becky, trying to smile. "They all seem to think it was you, Peter."

"They've got another think coming, then. I'll never pay a cent for that glass, and you can't make me." He approached her in the aisle, and glared at her threateningly. "My father'll back me up in it, too. He says if you get too fresh with me he'll show you what's what!"

"Take off your cap, and go back to your seat, Peter."

In the absence of Ole, Pete dared to defy authority. "Nobody's going to make me," he repeated.

"You'll either go back to your seat or else you'll go home."

"I'll not do neither one."

Becky hesitated a moment. She, too, realized that Ole was not there. But she had known for a long time that this conflict was bound to come, and that when it came she would have to meet it.

"You'll have to, Peter," she said firmly.

Pete had seen the hesitation, and knew that Becky was afraid. He advanced a step toward her with clenched fists and cloudy face.

Marietta, who was slower than the others, came through the outer door. "You ought to be ashamed of yourself, Pete Welp," she said. "Your sisters wouldn't be alive if it wasn't for the teacher."

Pete curved his backbone, in cruel imitation. "Shut up, Crip, or I'll break your humpy back," he growled.

All of the bottled-up wrath of the past year seethed inside of Becky. She had started school with the idea of letting bygones be bygones with the Welps, and in all these months she had never let fall any sign of her past resentment. But at the taunt to the crippled child the old fury that she had felt the day that Phil and Autie were lassoed came rushing over her. She understood how it was that civilization often dropped back into savagery. It was not kindness that could tame Pete Welp; it was justice that was needed — a rude, rough justice that he could understand. From that moment she knew that she must win in the battle of wills.

But Ole was not there. And Pete towered above her; the teacher would be a child in his hands. Strength could not be allowed to win; it must be a contest of wits. She withdrew a step or two as though frightened. Peter followed, menacingly. Becky stepped back farther, and again Peter followed. The girl gave a quick

glance toward the outside door, now only a yard
away. If Marietta had only left it ajar!

Step by step she backed toward it, as though
intimidated. Step by step Peter followed, his
face glowering, his fists ready. The little Wubbers shivered in their seats. Becky stretched out
her arm behind her, and felt for the knob of the
door. It was within her grasp. Pete brushed
Marietta aside and came closer. Becky swung
the door open wide, and, wheeling suddenly, gave
the half-grown boy a mighty push. He was head
and shoulders taller than she, but it was an unexpected assault. He was thrust through the doorway. Before he could turn back to the attack
twenty eager hands had banged the door shut,
and Becky turned the key in the lock.

Pete pounded at the door, but it stood firm.
Becky went directly to the lessons. Paying as
little attention as possible to the roars and threats
outside, she called out a class, and began the
arithmetic lesson. She felt sure that Pete could
not get into the room, and that his brother would
not attempt to get out and join him. Bill sat
with a tamed expression, and the two little Welp

girls cowered shamefacedly in their seats.

"Leave me in!" shouted Pete.

Becky shook the coal stove vigorously to drown out the noise, but gave no other evidence of attention.

"My father will make it hot for you! He'll show you if you can put me out o' school!"

"If your mother were cooking potatoes for your family of six, and she only had three potatoes, how would she divide them?" she asked Crystal.

"The baby don't eat potatoes," said the little girl.

"But suppose they all ate them, and your mother only had three, what would she do?"

Crystal was short on reasoning, but long on economy. "Mash 'em," said she. The school room filled with laughter which Pete, outside, felt was directed at him. He grew more noisy, and the lesson went on to the accompaniment of shrill catcalls, snowballs and threats, aimed at both teacher and schoolhouse. Becky tried to act as unconcerned as though that were a part of every day's program, but it was hard to get the children back to work. So it was a relief when wheels sounded outside, the catcalls stopped, and a procession of parents filed into the room. Mrs. Wubber led the way, carrying a large bundle which she set on Becky's table. Becky found chairs and empty desks for the other visitors, but Mrs. Wubber declined a seat. The children looked at her wide-eyed as she stepped to the front of the room, settled her hat more firmly, and addressed those assembled:

Ladies, gentlemen, childern, and Miss Linville:

When anything happens that is more than of average occurrence it is quite fitting that it be celebrated in some way. So it is with the Fourth of July and Christmas, which, while not much observed in this part of the country, is more observed in some other parts. Especially if there is a brave deed do we observe it with medals or monuments or other rewards.

We are here today, childern and fellow citizens, to rememberate a recent happening which was as brave as the winter in Valley Forge or the freeing of the slaves. I refer, as you all know, to the blizzard in Tripp County, which would have robbed us of our nearest and dearest if it had not been for the ee-nergy, the wisdom and the couringe of one person. Also the good horse-sense of that person, whom you all know.

Becky gave a little gasp. What was coming next.

The people of Tripp County are not rich in material wealth, but their hearts are true and they know a good deed when they see one. Also they know how to be grateful for favors, such as having their children restored to them with no damage but an empty stummick, after a night of sleepless worry on our parts.

We feel that such bravery and couringe should not go unnoticed and unrewarded. So we have asked small contributions from parents in this district, and I am glad to say that with but one exception, all compiled. With these funds we have purchased a slight token of our esteem, which I now take pleasure in presenting to your teacher, our friend, and the heroween of Tripp County — Miss Rebecca Linville.

The room rang with the applause. Mrs. Wubber wiped her hot face, and reached for the package on the table. She unwrapped the paper, and placed the contents in Becky's hands. It was a giant vase, over two feet high. A vase that in its past life had been covered with putty or plaster. Into this soft surface had been pressed such ornamental objects as marbles, screws, buttons, shells, tobacco tags, keys, cruet tops, and suspender buckles. These had been allowed to set, and the putty to harden, after which the vase had received a coat of bronze paint that gave a most regal effect to the commonplace articles embedded therein. Nothing more hideous could have been conceived, but the eyes of the homesteaders, as well as the children, glistened with admiration as they beheld its glories.

A year before the gift would have been comic to Becky. But now she saw only the friendship and the gratitude that had prompted it. She knew from what poverty-stricken homes had gone the pennies that had purchased it, and the pitiful stock from which a present could be selected in that homesteading country. There was real gratitude and tenderness in her voice as she tried to return thanks for the gift. The school work was stopped, and there was a program of music before the school was dismissed.

Mrs. Wubber, once off the lecture platform, became easy and colloquial. "We 'lowed you must be havin' trouble with those Welps, just as we came," she said. "That Pete was peltin' the school door good and proper. You should have seen him scuttle when we druv up."

Becky explained the discord of the afternoon. "It was I who put him out," she concluded with a sigh. "But I suppose the same trouble will start all over in the morning. He threatened to bring his father back and 'settle me.' I suppose I'm in for another fight, and I'm afraid there won't be another open door handy next time."

"You'll have no more trouble with the Welps," said Mr. Trainer, looking very pleased.

"Why not?"

"They're going to move away."

"When?"

"Soon as the roads are dry enough to freight their goods."

"Are you sure?"

"Dead sure," said Mr. Trainer. The other parents laughed. Everybody seemed pleased at something.

"Did Mr. Welp tell you he was going away to stay?"

"We told *him*," answered Mr. Lambert. "We men made a call on him on our way over here — a neighborly call, but a business one, too. We told him we didn't like his looks — his nor his family's — and that we'd decided that Tripp County air wasn't healthy for any of them. We thought he'd better move before any more cows got loose or children were abused; we were sick of seeing him pick on women and kids. He got fighting mad, of course, and said it was a free country; that he had this claim before you did, and he was going to keep it if he had to mortgage his soul for it."

"Lambert told him his soul was mighty poor security, and no bank would take it," put in Mr. Trainer.

"We all got after him, finally," said Mr. Lambert, "and told him that we weren't going to stand

for him any longer. That if he dared go on
with his contest we'd all get up and swear, lie or
no lie, that you Linvilles were here first; he
wouldn't get one neighbor to testify for him. We
mentioned, too, that tar and feathers could be
got hold of without any trouble, and that we'd
just about got to the tar and feather stage of the
game. We told him that we'd give him fifty
dollars for his shack — that's about forty-three
dollars more than it's worth — and that he'd have
to light out. He could decide than and there."

"And what did he do?" asked Becky, breathless
with suspense.

"Cussed us all round, kicked the cat, and finally
growled out that he'd go as soon as the roads
dried up. I believe he mentioned something
about not caring much for *his* neighbors, either,
but we didn't wait for his comments. We picked
up our women folks and came over here to cele-
brate."

"It's a wonderful celebration," said Becky.
"It's two gifts you've brought me, not one; my,
won't the Linvilles sleep well tonight!"

"A nice easy feeling all around," said Mr.

Trainer. "I guess there ain't much doubt, now, of our keeping our teacher."

The Wubbers offered Becky a seat in their wagon when the party started home, but she was not quite ready to leave. She sent the two children with them, waved a grateful good-by to the committee, and turned back to the schoolroom for a few last duties. She sang as she cleaned the blackboard, pushed back the desks and picked up the waste paper from the floor. The fear and menace of her life was gone now; she felt safe and happy. And that safety and happiness had been purchased by the fifty pieces of silver that had been given, a dime and a quarter at a time, by her poverty-stricken neighbors. They had come from homes where bread was needed, and potatoes; where there was no meat, and not enough heat, and insufficient clothes. Yet it had been given graciously and willingly — a grateful thank-offering from appreciative hearts.

Had it ever been that she thought the prairie an unfriendly place? That seemed years ago. It was *her* school now; her claim. Dakota was her home.

As she lifted Joan's spelling book to carry home with her, a paper fell out on the floor. Becky, picking it up, read :

The Welps they are so mene a lot
I wisch theyd die upon the spot
not both the grils that can not help
from being souch a thing as welp
But I wold be verry verry glad if bill and pete
wold be fond ded upon the strete.

Becky looked and laughed. "There's a better solution than that, Miss Joan," she said to the air. "Just wait until I get home and tell you!"

UNDER the prairie winds the roads dried quickly, and the following Sunday the Cleavers came over the Linville trail to congratulate Becky. She had become famous, said Mr. Cleaver, with a smile that held pride as well as fun; the *Dallas News* had not alone a story, but an editorial about her that had been copied everywhere in the state, and the history of her night in the blizzard had gone all over the country.

"Prairie Heroine Defies Elements," said Dick, with a grin.

"That'll be all from you, young man," replied Mr. Cleaver. "You can spend your time in being proud of that sister of yours. She's better known in South Dakota than I am after thirty years of residence here. Everybody's talking about her."

"Have you seen her vase?" asked Dick.

Becky threw a warning glance at him. Not even to the Cleavers would she admit that there was anything unbeautiful in that gift.

The children could not wait to tell that the Welp family were leaving the neighborhood. "That's what we're celebrating today," said Becky. "Dick killed a chicken for us, and we're *not* going to have turnip or prunes! In other words, it's a holiday. How lucky you happened along when it's roast chicken instead of eggs served in a frying pan."

Mr. Cleaver went out with Dick to see the work that had been done on the dam during the last days of fall. He had built a wall across the creek-bed, plastered the cracks, and built an overflow for the water. "I didn't have much heart in the work when I started it," he explained. "I was afraid I was doing it for the Welps. But that worry's over now."

"You'll have a real lake here when the ice melts," said Mr. Cleaver.

"That's what I'm after," said the boy. "Beck misses the trees an awful lot. *I* never think of that part of Platteville, but you know how girls are: they'll put up with all kinds of trouble without a word, and then go dippy over missing a hill. Just as soon as the frost gets out of the ground I'm going to move up a few cottonwoods and an ash from the thicket, and Mr. Dennison is going to send me some cedars and a couple of hard maples from home. I think they'll grow near the water. Becky never could get over the birds trying to find shade behind the fence posts, last summer, and I'm going to see that she has a little herself when it gets a hundred in the shade. She was a pretty good scout last year, and hot weather is fierce on her, too."

"Your fourteen months will be up next summer."

"Yes, the last of next July."

"Are you going to be able to meet your payments?"

"Yes, we're all right now — if nobody's sick. We have new tenants in the Platteville house, and with Beck teaching school we'll be on Easy Street. It won't be long now before I can help."

"You don't seem to have been exactly idle all the time you've been out here. What will you do after your fourteen months are up? Think you'd be satisfied to stay on in Dakota?"

Dick looked abashed, but pleased at the praise. "Sure," he answered. "I didn't feel that way last summer, when things looked so black. But living's easier now, and it gets easier every day. The kids look better than they ever did before in their lives — I guess we all do — and we're learning how to get along better. I'd like to stay and see what we can make out of the place as a farm, not a claim. We've just got things started to work for us, and it's fun to see how they turn out. But the staying's up to Beck."

"Is she lonely for Platteville?"

"Well, I don't know what to say. She loves

this place more than I do, I believe. You know
Becky; she can get drunk on a sunset. But she
doesn't get over Uncle Jim. She says she left
him behind in Platteville; that he's never
seemed to be out here with us. Of course she
doesn't kick about living here — Beck never says
she's lonesome — but I know just the same. It's
Uncle Jim she wants, though, more than Platteville."

Mr. Cleaver laid his fur glove on the shoulder
of Dick's canvas coat. "I can't understand why
two nice people like Mrs. Cleaver and me
couldn't have had four nice kids like you," he
said.

In the house Mrs. Cleaver was helping Joan
set the table, while Becky thickened the cream
sauce for the gravy. "Put on the tablecloth with
the monogram," ordered Becky. "Get the Swope
plate for the bread, open the jar of spiced cherries from home, and throw the nicked cup into
the ash can. Let us dine as befitting our station
in life — school-teacher for another year, and
almost-owners of a claim! I wish I didn't have
to open another can. When we have proved up,

and get our homestead receipts I shall never eat another canned pea."

"Peas aren't so bad as turnips," observed Joan.

"Well, perhaps I won't renounce the pea until I know how the crops turn out, next year. But oh, Mrs. Cleaver, I've eaten my way through a billion tin cans this year. I have real admiration for the grit and persistence of the goat."

Mrs. Cleaver laughed, but there was a note of sympathy in her voice.

"I felt just that way, too, when I first came to Dakota. But things won't be so unappetizing after you get your own garden. Shall I mash the potatoes now?"

"Rap on the window for the men, Joan," said Becky. "We'll be ready by the time Dick washes his hands."

"Dick's not a man," said the little girl.

"He seems that way to me," said Becky. "Knock hard, so they'll hear you."

Joan stepped to the window. "Who's that driving by?" she asked. "Look at the load of goods. Someone's freighting on Sunday. Why, Becky, it's the Welps!"

Mrs. Cleaver and the three children looked out of the window between the sash curtains. Two thin horses were pulling the Welp wagon over the trail. It was loaded with shabby household goods. Mr. Welp and his two boys sat on the front seat; in the wagon box were Mrs. Welp and the two other children. The little girls looked wistfully at the house as they passed. Mrs. Welp kept her eyes fastened on the chair she was steadying, the boys looked straight ahead, and Mr. Welp aimed a blow at Bronx as they passed.

"I'd like to aim a turnip at *him!*" said Joan.

The horses strained under the load, the wagon jolted over the ruts in the frozen trail, and across the gray prairie the Welps passed out of the sight and the life of the Linvilles.

"Good-by to nothing," remarked Phil, as the wagon melted into the trail.

"I'm sorry for that poor woman," said Becky. "We're rid of him, but she's got him for life."

"It's her own fault," said Joan. "You got to stop and think before you pick out a husband."

Dinner, and dishes, and a gay afternoon with the Cleavers.

"It's just like Platteville when you come," said Joan. "Wish you could stay here. Then it would seem like home."

"Seems like home to us," said Mr. Cleaver. "Every time we get lonesome for kids we're coming out here. Look out for us every ten days or so."

When the guests were ready to go they called Becky's attention to a basket that they were leaving behind. "Can't you come without bearing gifts?" asked Becky.

"It's nothing but junk," was Mrs. Cleaver's comment.

"Don't miss the photograph in the white envelope," said Mr. Cleaver. "I found it going through my old films last week; I'd forgotten that I ever took it."

"Who is it?" inquired Becky curiously. "Hope it's Mrs. Cleaver."

"You'll see," said her guest. "Come on out, you young fry, and open the gate for us."

THE sun was low in the sky when their visitors drove away, and Becky ceased to wave from the

window. The children had stayed in the barn
to gather the eggs, and Dick was milking Red
Haw. That would give her a chance to open the
basket before the family came in. She carried
it to the window to get the light of the sun. It was
sinking fast now, the clouds were white islands
in a sea of fire.

Becky opened the hamper. A layer of oranges and apples, each one wrapped to prevent
freezing; some "ready-to-sew" dresses for Joan;
a puzzle game; a pile of magazines; two late nov-
els, and a box of real Omaha chocolates. And
down in the bottom the white envelope. Becky
took out the kodak picture and held it close up to
the window.

It was Uncle Jim; not the Uncle Jim of Platteville, but the Uncle Jim of the prairies. He was
standing near the creek-bed, against a background of leafless wild plum branches. His
flannel shirt was open at the throat, and the wind
was blowing his hair. There were smile wrinkles
around his eyes, but he was not smiling. He was
looking away across the sea of grass with an expression on his face that was intense, tender, and

almost rapt.   It was as though someone he loved had called to him, and he had lifted his head to reply.

Tears shut away the picture, but they were not tears of bitterness.   For as Becky looked, she knew that the prairie was Uncle Jim's home. He, too, had heard its call to stay, and she knew from his face what his answer would be.